THE BLUE BUTTERFLY

A Liz Lucas Cozy Mystery - Book 5

BY

DIANNE HARMAN

Published by: Dianne Harman
www.dianneharman.com

Interior, cover design and website by
Vivek Rajan Vivek
www.vivekrajanvivek.com

ISBN: 978-1523406197

CONTENTS

ACKNOWLEDGMENTS

To each and every one of my readers, I sincerely thank you. You have made my books best sellers beyond my dreams. When I started writing cozy mysteries, I had no idea I would write three series and be in the process of starting a fourth, the Midwest Cozy Mystery Series. Without loyal readers like you, I wouldn't be a successful writer. It's as simple as that. My husband recently asked me which of my books was my favorite. I looked at him in shock and replied, "They're my children. I love each and every one of them equally."

I would be remiss if I didn't acknowledge my writing Muse who often visits me in the middle of the night, depriving me of sleep, and helping me work out plots and plan for my next book. I've come to appreciate her input (for some reason I'm sure my Muse is a female!)

There are two people I've come to rely on during this writing journey of mine, my husband, Tom, and my friend, Vivek Rajan. Tom patiently reads each book several times and lets me know when I've made a mistake in a character's name or time inconsistencies or anything else I've missed. He's also great at coming up with plot twists and fleshing out characters. Vivek is responsible for the book covers and the formatting – things I'm more than happy to have him do. He's also been indispensable when it comes to media marketing. I'm a believer that no one is going to look under a rock for my books. He helps me give them visibility. Thanks to both of you!

Lastly, to my boxer dog Kelly, who has finally become the dog I'd hoped for when I got her. She recently had her first birthday, so thankfully the puppy stage has pretty much ended. I think she topped it off when she ate part of our couch, and it's going to have to be recovered! It's wonderful not to have to stop writing to see why she's quiet or wondering what she's doing. Many a house plant has suffered from her curiosity. In retrospect, Nature Girl probably would have been a better name for her because she tends to bury her toys in the house plants! Thanks Kelly for letting me write!

Amazing Ebooks & Paperbacks for FREE

Go to www.dianneharman.com/freepaperback.html and get your FREE copies of Dianne's books and Dianne's favorite recipes immediately by signing up for her newsletter.

Once you've signed up for her newsletter you're eligible to win autographed paperbacks. One lucky winner is picked every week. Hurry before the offer ends.

PROLOGUE

The Lotis Blue butterfly has not been seen since 1983 and is considered to be rarest butterfly in North America. With a wingspan of only one inch, it's a beautiful little butterfly with a deep violet-blue color on its wing surface. It was last seen in a few remote coastal bogs not far from Mendocino on California's north coast. It's on the U.S. Endangered Species List.

CHAPTER ONE

"Roger, I have to go into town today. How about meeting me at Gertie's Diner for lunch? I've got a craving for one of her hamburgers and a chocolate malt," Liz Langley said to her husband.

"You know you don't have to ask me twice. Consider it done. Renting the space next door to her diner may not have been the smartest thing I've ever done. I think I've gained ten pounds in the six months since we got married, and I moved my law practice from San Francisco to here in Red Cedar. Between you and Gertie, I can kiss my former slender fit body goodbye."

"Roger, I think that slender fit body label was a figment of your imagination. Not that I'm complaining, but keep one thing in mind. Neither Gertie nor I is forcing you to eat. The hand that takes the fork from the plate to the mouth is none other than your own," she said with a hint of laughter in her voice. "Anyway, I need to go shopping at the market. It looks like the next couple of weeks will be pretty busy here at the spa."

Liz was the owner of the Red Cedar Spa and Lodge, a very popular getaway for people from the San Francisco area, and with the recent publicity about the spa's mascot, a St. Bernard dog named Brandy Boy, the clientele was now coming from all over the west coast. The attractive widow with the auburn hair, full figure, and sea-green eyes had recently married Roger Langley, a criminal law attorney who worked at the San Francisco law firm that handled the probate of her late husband's estate.

Roger looked at his watch. "Would love to stay and talk, sweetheart, but if I don't leave now I'll have a client waiting on the sidewalk, and that certainly won't help when I quote my fee to him. Take care of her, Winston," Roger said, patting the big boxer dog that stood next to Liz in his usual protective mode.

He leaned down and kissed Liz. "Love you," he said as he walked out the door. "See you at noon."

Just as Liz closed the door behind him she heard her phone ringing. She looked at the monitor and saw that it was Gertie. "Gertie, you must be telepathic. Roger and I were just talking about meeting for lunch at your diner. I'm hungry for one of your hamburgers and a chocolate malt."

"Ya' know yer' always welcome at the diner, honey. I'll make sure ya' get enuf' to eat, so you'll be full as a tick. Got a favor to ask of ya'."

"Sure, what can I do for you?"

"Well, don't talk about my family much, but I got a brother, actually he's a step-brother, who's about twenty years younger'n me. He works fer the California Forestry Service, doin' somethin' or other, but I never could figger out what it is. Anyway, he's drivin' over to Red Cedar today and asked if I knew someplace he could stay. I thought of you and wondered if ya' got a cottage there at the spa he could use fer a few days beginnin' tonight. He squeezes a quarter so tight the eagle screams, but he can sure afford it. Been tellin' him fer years that sometimes the squeeze ain't worth the juice. Don't think it registers with him."

"Gertie, I don't know if anything's available. Let me check with Bertha, and I'll get right back to you."

"Thanks, honey. Appreciate it. Talk to ya' later."

Kelly pressed the intercom on her desk and said, "Bertha, I just had a call from Gertie. Her step-brother's going to be in town for a few days, and she wondered if we had an opening in one of our cottages."

"Must be Gertie's lucky day. I just received a cancellation from a woman in Los Angeles. She'd planned her spa trip months ago, but her elderly mother broke her hip yesterday, and she had to cancel her trip. Do you want me to call Gertie, or do you want to?" Bertha, Liz's long-time spa manager, asked.

"I'll give her a call. I'm going into town, and Roger and I are planning on meeting for lunch at Gertie's Diner. Before I leave I'll pick up the key from you and give it to her for her step-brother. She didn't say when he was coming into town."

"I'll put the key on my desk in case I'm not here when you come to the office. I need to spend some time at the spa. I have some interviews scheduled today for people who have applied to work here. We need to add a couple of massage therapists and facialists."

"As always, Bertha, thanks. See you later."

She pressed Gertie's cell number on her phone and a moment later heard Gertie say, "That was fast, lady. What's the answer?"

"The spa just had a cancellation," Liz said. "We'd love to have your step-brother stay here. The woman who cancelled had booked the cottage for a week, so that should give him plenty of time to do whatever it is he needs to do. When I come to the diner for lunch today I'll bring the key, and you can give it to him. Gertie, I'm a little curious. I know it's none of my business, but why isn't he going to stay with you, if you don't mind me asking?"

"Don't mind none at all, honey. Probably jaw 'bout stuff like that too much as it is. Like I said earlier, we're 'bout twenty years apart. My mother divorced my dad and then re-married. Her new husband had a son named David Sanders, and he became my step-brother and is the one who's coming to town today. My mother's new husband was bucks up, and when he died he left it all to my mother. And then ten years later when my mother died, she left it to me. Never did set real well with David. He kinda' thinks that money my mom left to me mostly came from his father, so it shoulda' gone to him, not me. Think it's better if we don't stay in the same house. Old hurt feelin's and all, ya' know."

"I'm sorry, Gertie. I feel like I know you well, but then again, I guess we never know much about someone else unless they want to tell us. I'll see you at noon. I have one last question. If you two aren't that close, why is he coming here?"

"Danged if I know. Said somethin' 'bout a blue butterfly. Guy always was a little strange. I mean, why'd anyone travel all the way from Sacramento because of a blue butterfly? Don't make no sense to me."

"Me neither. See you at lunch."

Liz put the phone down and looked out the window at the sparkling blue ocean and the constant activity that went on both in it and above it. Sea gulls circled overhead, diving and twisting as they rode the air currents looking for a morsel of food on the ocean's surface. The day was blustery and white caps constantly shifted and changed the look of the ocean's surface. It was as if the ocean was a living thing, a scene that never failed to enchant her. She often felt she must be one of the most fortunate people in the world to be able to live high above the ocean and watch the play of nature taking place in front of her.

An added bonus during this time of the year was catching sight of pods of grey whales as they migrated from Mexico to Alaska. She often saw them when their migratory path brought them closer to shore. It never failed to thrill her, but it wasn't to be today. The whales were either farther north or farther south, but today none of them were in the ocean in front of the Red Cedar Spa.

CHAPTER TWO

Liz took the sacks of food she'd bought at the market and put them in the back of her van. After they were loaded, she got in and drove the few blocks to Gertie's Diner. "Winston, you stay here. I'll be about an hour. Here's some water, and I've put the window down for you. Guard the car, boy."

A few moments later she walked into Gertie's Diner. She was greeted by Gertie, the owner, who was a throwback to another era with her bleached blond hair piled in a tall beehive, five inch high stiletto heels, lips smacking with her ever present wad of bubble gum, and a pencil stuck behind her ear. Even though she looked like she belonged in a bygone era, Gertie had a heart of gold, and once you were her friend, you were her friend for life. While her malted milk shakes and hamburgers were legendary, with people coming from as far away as San Francisco which was about an hour south of Red Cedar, her warm personality was even more legendary. Although Liz wasn't really sure why the diner was so popular with customers, she was pretty sure many of them came not only for the food but to bask in the warmth of Gertie, the loving non-conformist owner of the diner.

"Roger's over there waitin' fer ya'. Refused to order 'til ya' got here. What a gentleman," Gertie said as she motioned to a booth that was near the entrance to the kitchen. "Know what yer' thinkin' Liz, ain't the best seat in the house, but honey, it was the only seat left when he got here. Better to eat sittin' than standin' I always say. Be with ya' in a minute."

Roger stood up when Liz walked over to the booth and gave her a hug. "So how was your new client?" Liz asked as she gave the waitress her menu and said, "We already know what we want, right Roger?"

"Yep. I know I should make it past the hamburger and malted milk shake, but it's not going to happen today," he said looking up at the shiny-faced young teenage girl who had just started working at Gertie's. "Make that a double order, one for my wife and one for me." The young girl wrote down their order and walked through the swinging kitchen doors. Liz heard sounds of laughter and talking coming from the kitchen staff.

A few minutes later Gertie walked over to their booth and sat down. "Ya' got that key fer my brother? He's in the kitchen, and I'll give it to him. He said somethin' 'bout gettin' a bite to eat and then headin' out to do some work. Told him he could either eat dinner here or out at yer' lodge, but he said he didn't think he'd make it back in time for dinner with ya'. Glad ya' were comin' to town, so he can get the key and not have to bother ya' late tonite."

"Here it is. He'll be in cottage number one. It's easy to find, because it's the first one you come to when you get to the end of the lane. Please tell him I look forward to meeting him."

"Will do. You two lovebirds have a nice lunch, and I'll see ya' later. Need to work the room a little. Ya' know what that's like," she said winking. "Keep thinkin' of yer friend Bob, that new County Supervisor, and how he and his wife can work a room. Lawdy, went to a fundraiser for him and never seen nothin' like it. Took a few lessons from them I did," she said leaving the booth and greeting the people at the table across from it. After stopping briefly at every table in the diner, she walked back into the kitchen.

When Roger had finished the last bite of his burger he rubbed his hand over his stomach and said, "I'm glad you cook healthier than this, although sometimes a man just needs to surrender to his animal instincts, and this certainly is one of mine."

"Been my experience that's not the only animal instinct you're capable of indulging in, Roger," Liz said, laughing.

"Careful what you say, lady. I've got my downtown image to protect here."

"Right," she said, rolling her eyes heavenward. She cocked her head, suddenly aware of angry voices coming from the kitchen. "Roger, do you hear that? It sounds like Gertie, and she seems to be very angry." Liz realized the other diners had stopped talking, and many of them were looking towards the kitchen, obviously having heard the angry voices being raised in what sounded like an argument.

Liz, Roger, and the other diners clearly heard a loud male voice shout, "You know you stole it from me. You made your mother give it to you, and you made sure that she left me out of her Will. Well, I hope you're happy. If it hadn't been for my father's money, you never would have been able to open up this dirt bag rinky-dink diner."

"That's not true. I saved everything I could to open it up. Had nothin' to do with ya' or yer' father," a voice that sounded like Gertie's responded.

"Sure you did. You're just as blind to that as you were to all the loser husbands you had that you spent my dad's money on."

"Get outta my kitchen," Gertie angrily shouted. "This is my diner, and I want ya' to get out now."

"Roger, I'm going back there. This is so unlike Gertie. The way they're yelling at each other it could get dangerous for her. She's my friend, and I want to make sure she's all right," Liz said, sliding out of the booth and hurrying through the swinging doors leading to the kitchen.

Gertie was standing in the middle of the kitchen, the staff having moved to the sides. She was glaring at a handsome large man with a black beard and bright blue eyes wearing a uniform of green pants and a grey shirt with a California Forestry Service patch sewn on the left sleeve of the shirt.

"Gertie, is everything all right?" Liz asked.

Gertie pulled her attention away from the man and said, "David here likes to holler like a stuck pig. Ain't no truth to what he's sayin'. Always did like to hear hisself talk." She threw the key to cottage number one at him. "This here's Liz, the owner of the Red Cedar Spa and Lodge where you'll be stayin' tonight. Can't miss it. Take the road north out of town. It's about a mile. Big sign. You're in cottage number one. Now git out 'afore I do somethin' I might regret, but probably wouldn't."

The big man caught the key and stormed out through the back door of the diner, slamming it behind him. "So what are ya' all lookin' at? Get back to work. We gots a lot of people out there who are hungry," Gertie said to her staff who were staring at her wide-eyed. They'd never seen this side of Gertie, and they were obviously shocked at what they'd just witnessed. They drifted back to what they'd been doing before the angry exchange of raised voices had taken place, and soon the kitchen returned to normal.

"Gertie, the voices of you and your step-brother were quite loud, and I'm sure some of the people out in the seating area heard the two of you arguing. Do you want me to do anything?"

"Nah, sometimes David thinks the sun comes up just to hear him crow. Nothin' to what he said. Jes' old words from a long time ago. He can't let it go. Guess he thinks if it weren't for mom and me he'd be livin' in high cotton. Never ya' mind, ya' ain't got no dog in this hunt. That boy could start an argument in an empty house. No wonder he can never hold onta' a woman. Ain't got no whaddya call it? Think the word's finesse."

Liz turned around and walked out of the kitchen. She could see that people had gone on to other things, and the incident in the kitchen between Gertie and her step-brother had been forgotten as they began to discuss whatever the next most importance thing was to them.

"Well, what did you find out?" Roger asked with a worried look on his face as she scooted back into the booth. She told him about the conversation she'd had earlier in the day with Gertie and then answered his question.

"I guess it confirms there isn't a lot of love lost between Gertie and her step-brother. Strange thing. When I asked her earlier why he'd come to Red Cedar if they didn't get along, she said he'd mentioned something about a blue butterfly. That's kind of weird. I mean I know he's with the Forestry Service, so maybe he has something to do with butterflies, but I can't figure out what that would be."

"Are you sure that's what she said?" Roger asked.

"Yes, why?"

"We've had conversations about coincidences before, and how I don't believe in them. Well, this is certainly a coincidence considering I just had a conversation with a client about a butterfly called the Lotis Blue butterfly."

CHAPTER THREE

"Ruby, did you know David Sanders is in Red Cedar?" George Myers angrily shouted as he threw open the front door of their home.

"Of course not. Why would he be here?"

"Probably to see if you'll take him back. Did he call you or what?"

"No," Ruby said with her hands on her hips and the color in her cheeks starting to match the color of her long curly red hair. "I haven't seen David since the day I walked out on him in Sacramento nearly two years ago. You know that. I can't believe what you're insinuating. Anyway, what makes you think he's in town?"

"I know we usually have lunch here at the house, so I thought I'd go to Gertie's Diner and get a couple of hamburgers to go for us for lunch. When I got to the diner I saw a Forestry Service car parked in front of it. Figured it wasn't a coincidence that since David is Gertie's step-brother, the car had to belong to him. I know it could have been one of the other Forestry Service people, but I sat in my car and waited until he came out the back door. He looked really angry when he got in the car. I recognized him from some of those photos I saw of you and him, the ones I threw out after we got married. Yeah, it was David Sanders all right. I kind of remember you telling me how he and Gertie didn't get along real well."

"That's the understatement of the year, but you have to believe me, George. I haven't had any communication with David for two years. He was part of my past, and you know those days are over. Even my mom can tell you that."

"Your mom would say anything to protect you so forget about having her come to your rescue. David may be part of your past, but you're still an employee of the Forestry Service and so is he. Since he's here he'll probably go to the local Forestry Service office, and you'll see him. How do you plan on handling that situation?"

"I have no idea. Maybe there's something going on at the office I don't know about and that's why he's here. When I left for lunch, Les told me he wanted me in the office this afternoon and not out in the field, because he was holding a meeting at 2:00, and he wanted all the staff there. I have no idea what it's about. Maybe it has something to do with why David's in town."

"Ruby, you know I've worked real hard to control those anger issues I used to have. I've been seeing Dr. Lewis every week just like you told me I had to do before you agreed to marry me, but so help me, if David Sanders tries anything with you, I'll kill him."

"George, don't even say something like that. It scares me, and it's not funny. You've done so well with Dr. Lewis, and you know those anger issues were the only thing standing in the way of our getting married. When Dr. Lewis told me you'd been able to get your anger under control and deal with it in a normal manner, that's when I told you I'd marry you. Believe me, I wouldn't do anything that would cause you to have problems like you used to have."

He glowered at her and clenched his fists. "Ruby, I'm telling you, if he looks at you or if he touches you, I'll kill him. He's old enough to be your father. I never could understand why you were ever involved with him in the first place. Maybe you've got some daddy issues or something you need to talk to Dr. Lewis about, but you're mine now, not his. You remember that, and if he even thinks of doing anything, you tell him I'll be the last person he'll ever see. Understand what I'm saying?"

"Yes, baby, I understand. You don't need to worry. You're the one I love, not David Sanders." She walked over to George and put her arms around him. "I wouldn't do anything to jeopardize what we have, you know that."

"I'd like to believe you, but when a guy from your past comes into town and you both work for the same employer, I don't like it."

"I don't blame you, but David Sanders means nothing to me other than a name from my past."

"Good. Make sure you keep it that way," he said, roughly kissing her.

She returned his kiss and then pushed him away. "I've got to get back to office. I'm probably going to be late as it is. See you tonight."

So David's in town. Wonder what he wants. I'd never admit it to George, but I would like to see David and talk to him. Just for old times' sake, Ruby thought. *Maybe he'll be at the meeting this afternoon. George won't be there, and anyway, he'd never know about it if I talked to David.*

CHAPTER FOUR

"Liz, let's go over to my office. I've got a couple of things relating to the law office I'd like to run by you, and one of them involves the blue butterfly Gertie mentioned to you. I don't like to discuss things that relate to my law practice in a restaurant. Rather doubt anyone would care what we're talking about, but it will make me feel better if we discuss them in the privacy of my office. My next appointment isn't for an hour. Would that be okay with you, or do you have something you have to do right away?"

"No. I do need to get back to the lodge, unpack the groceries, and get organized for dinner, but I have a little time. Let's go."

The young waitress had left their bill on a brown tray which she'd put on their table. Roger dropped some cash in it, stood up, and said, "She was a good waitress. I don't mind tipping people who are really trying to do a good job even if they are new at it." A few minutes later Liz and Roger were in his office, Roger behind his desk, and Liz sitting in a client chair across from him.

"So, Roger, what's this about? You mentioned there were a couple of things you wanted to talk to me about."

"One of my law firm's clients is Jefferson Lumber Company which is headquartered here in Red Cedar. When I opened the firm's branch office here the firm suggested to Lewis Jefferson, the owner of the company, that it would be much easier for him to come to the office in Red Cedar when his company had legal problems rather than drive down to San Francisco. He readily agreed. Naturally, I've met him a number of times in San Francisco, but today was the first time he's come to my office."

"I don't think you've ever mentioned his name to me, but since your expertise is in criminal law, why would you be meeting with him?" Liz asked.

"You're absolutely right. Criminal law has always been my specialty, but when the firm decided I should open this office, it was agreed I'd have to expand my practice into other areas of law. Let's face it. If I looked solely to the residents of Red Cedar to provide me with enough clients who had criminal problems we'd starve, and I wouldn't even be able to pay the rent. While there have been a couple of murders here, there really isn't much crime in this sleepy little town.

"As you know, we have attorneys in the firm who specialize in all kinds of law, so when I opened this office, my partners told me I had carte blanche to use the expertise of those attorneys whenever I needed to. Anyway, it's not surprising I've never mentioned Lewis to you. A couple of my partners handled most of his business. I knew sooner or later he'd probably come in to see me, because a company as large as his is constantly having legal problems of one kind or another. That's simply a fact of life, and Lewis is astute enough to realize when he needs to get legal help. He called me last week and made an appointment to see me. He said he had a couple of things he needed to talk to me about."

"Well, now my curiosity is definitely aroused. What were those things?"

"He showed me an unsigned letter he'd recently received. Whoever wrote it said that several people familiar with butterflies had spotted a Lotis Blue butterfly on one of Jefferson's timber properties and had photographs to prove it. The letter said that the Lotis Blue butterfly is on the Endangered Species List and prior to this alleged sighting hasn't been seen since 1983. It went on to say that if all logging wasn't immediately stopped in the area where the butterfly was observed, several people were willing to take the steps necessary to stop the logging. The content of the letter was quite threatening, and Lewis was concerned not only for himself, but for his employees who were working in that area. He's very aware of the power environmentalists can wield if they want to, and from the tone of the letter, they definitely want to."

"How does that work?"

"They would go to court and get an order to stop all logging activities because of the sighting of the butterfly. If they really do have photographs, they might be able to get a judge to grant a restraining order, since this particular butterfly is on the Endangered Species List," Roger said.

"Does that mean that all logging would stop right then and there?"

"Yes, and it's important to understand that Lewis is a very caring employer. He's not only concerned about the amount of money his company would lose on a daily basis if the logging had to be stopped, but he's also worried about what would happen to his employees if a restraining order is granted by the court. He knows he can't keep them on the payroll if no money is coming in from logging operations. His company is one of the few lumber companies that's been able to hang on during these last few years because of the slowdown in the economy and new environmental restrictions on logging activities. Lumber towns and the whole industry have all suffered tremendously."

"That's horrible. Can you do anything about it?"

"Not until whoever sent the letter decides to go public. As of now no one has served my client with a cease and desist order, and until that happens we're simply in a wait and see mode."

"Do you think Gertie's step-brother came here because of the

Lotis Blue butterfly? Maybe the person who wrote the letter tipped off the Forestry Service."

"That's a possibility. Maybe her step-brother wanted to see for himself if there are any here, but he'd be in a real quandary, because the Forestry Service is charged with the responsibility of protecting the resources of the state, and the forests of California are certainly a resource and a huge resource that provides much needed tax revenue to the state."

"Roger, let me see if I understand what you're saying. Are you telling me that if the presence of the Lotis Blue butterfly is threatening to shut down a lumber company the Forestry Service would oppose such a shutdown?"

"That would be my initial interpretation of the situation. Stay tuned because it may get very interesting. When these enviro activists get involved in something, they can sure make life miserable for the companies or people who oppose them.

"The other thing that Lewis wanted to talk to me about is quite confidential, Liz, but of course you know anything I tell you is confidential. Evidently one of the plant managers at Jefferson Lumber got a little careless with some formaldehyde that was being used at their plywood production plant. Lewis told me this particular plant specializes in producing outdoor and marine plywood which requires the application of formaldehyde to combat high humidity. Anyway, at least one of the men at the plant has developed cancer. Lewis is concerned he'll sue Jefferson Lumber Company."

"I didn't know people could get cancer from working in a plywood plant."

"Lewis told me it's quite common and happens when appropriate safety measures aren't taken to protect the workers. Evidently this plant manager didn't take the necessary steps to do that. Lewis isn't sure what he's going to do about the plant manager, because he's always considered him to be one of his best employees."

"I think your hands may be very full with several legal problems in the near future. I'd love to stay and talk, but I need to get those groceries back to the lodge. See you later. Looks like all the cottages are full tonight, so I want you to be on your best behavior at dinner," she said grinning as she stood up.

"I promise I'll be utterly charming to all of the guests. Give Winston a pat on the head for me. By the way, what's for dinner tonight?"

"You just finished a huge hamburger and malt. I can't believe you're even thinking about food."

"I told you I can't help it. I have animal instincts when it comes to food."

"Yeah. I think we talked about you and your animal instincts a little while ago. Okay, we're having roasted pork loin with mashed potatoes and a vegetable. Haven't decided what the vegetable will be yet, but I can promise you a fabulous Neopolitan ice cream dish with a strawberry balsamic sauce."

Roger looked at her and slowly lowered his head onto his desk. Liz could barely make out what his muffled voice was saying, but it sounded like, "I think I've died and gone to heaven."

"Ciao. Try to recover and get ready for your next appointment. Clients don't trust lawyers who conduct business while drooling with their head on their desk." She closed the door behind her and smiled at the man who was in the reception area, obviously Roger's next client.

A few minutes later, she patted Winston on the head as she got in her van and said, "That's from Roger." The big dog wagged his tail as if he understood everything that was being said.

CHAPTER FIVE

"Trace, I'm glad you called. I really miss not being in class. What is this all about, and why did you want to come out here?" Olivia asked the young man with the butterfly net attached to his belt.

"I heard there was a Lotis Blue butterfly spotted on this tract of timber. It's on the Endangered Species List, and I wanted to see if I could find it. If I could find one, not only would I be helping an endangered species, it would sure help me with my master's degree and it would make applying for the doctorate degree program a lot easier." He stopped talking and was quiet for a moment.

"Wait, look over there on that green bush," he said excitedly. "I think I see one. I can't believe it. I thought maybe when those people said they'd seen one in this area it was a figment of their imagination. I even wondered if they'd taken a picture of one from some book, but look, it's for real. I don't think I've ever been so excited. I can't see it now, because it flew farther back into the forest, but I'm sure that's what I saw."

"I know how important the environment is to you, Trace, and thanks for asking me to come out here to share this with you. This could be huge for your career at the university. I think there's a problem, though, because I hear chainsaws. Jefferson Lumber must be cutting trees down somewhere nearby. This area may be next."

Trace cocked his ear. "You're right. Those are definitely the sounds of chainsaws. That's what they use to cut down big trees like these. If they clear-cut this area, it means the Lotis Blue butterfly is going to lose its habitat. We've got to do something to get them to stop cutting the trees down. I know the Forestry Service in Sacramento was notified, but I'm not sure if they'd do anything to help. They're more concerned about managing the state's resources than saving endangered species. Sounds like a real conflict of interest to me," he said.

"What should we do? Something's got to be done immediately, or the trees will be gone, and so will the butterfly's home. This is exactly why I changed my major to Environmental Sciences. I want to help preserve things for future generations. This is just so wrong," Olivia said with a rising sound of alarm in her voice.

"I agree, but I don't think we have the luxury of waiting even a day or two. What do you think?" Trace asked.

"I really didn't know anything about the Lotis Blue butterfly until you called me yesterday, but I don't want to see their habitat destroyed. I know how important environmental things are to you, and I have to say, they've become very important to me even though there's not much I can do about them right now."

They heard a car pull into the parking lot that was used by both day hikers and by the lumbermen working in the area. "I hear someone coming," he said. "If the person is with the lumber company, we could be in trouble for trespassing. I think you better go to your car and get out of here. I'm going to catch that butterfly, and then maybe I can stop them from cutting down any more trees."

"Do you think you can catch it, Trace?" Olivia asked.

"I don't know, but I've got to try. I brought my net with me, and I'm going to go farther back into the forest. I may not be back for a little while," he said, taking the net from his belt where it hung. "Go ahead without me. Whoever was in the car we heard won't be able to find me. I've got to get that butterfly. Even though it doesn't know it, an entire species is depending on me." He ran down the forest path and never looked back at her.

Olivia waited for a few minutes to see if he'd return. She glanced at her watch and realized she needed to get home. When she got to the parking lot, no one was there. She looked back to where she'd last seen Trace and thought, *I would have sworn Trace had light brown eyes. I can remember thinking how beautiful they were when he was teaching that environmental class I took from him at UC Berkeley, before I had to quit a few months ago because of mom's heart surgery. Strange. He must really be excited about this butterfly because, he sure didn't seem like himself today.*

CHAPTER SIX

"Hi, Mom. I'm home. How are you feeling?" Olivia asked the woman who was lying on a couch in the living room with a blanket wrapped around her.

"I'm fine, honey. Don't worry about me. I'm sure I'll feel better soon. The doctor said that being tired after heart surgery is pretty common. I'm just not used to it. Ever since your father died, I've pretty much done everything around here, and having no energy is a strange feeling for me. I feel so bad about you dropping out of Berkeley. I know how much you enjoyed going there, and whenever you called you mentioned how exciting the environmental classes were and how much you enjoyed them."

"Mom, you know you, Cissy, and Amber are more important to me than finishing college. Next year I'll probably go to the small college that's over in Joplin. I can live here while I finish my degree there. Anyway, with you out of work, money's a little tight. I know we're pretty much living on what grandma and grandpa left you when they died, but at some point that's going to run out. I don't want to be the one responsible for using up all your money just so I could go to Berkeley. By the way, where are Cissy and Amber? They should be home from school by now."

"Mrs. Nichols called and asked if they could go home with her daughter, Jenna. She said Jenna gets lonesome now that her sister's married and left town. She'll bring them home after dinner."

"Good. This hasn't been easy for them, either."

"I know. I feel bad for all of you. Where did you go this afternoon?"

"I think I told you in one of my phone calls from Berkeley that a teaching assistant, Trace Logan, and I had become friends. He called last night and asked if I could meet him and then show him where the Jefferson Lumber Company property was located. He said an endangered species had been spotted there, the Lotis Blue butterfly. I told him I'd meet him in front of Gertie's Diner. I figured if he got lost someone would be able to give him directions to it, because it's kind of an institution in this town."

Olivia's mother looked up at her and smiled. "Is he a friend like a regular friend, or is he a special friend?"

"Mom, it wasn't anything like that. He really is just a friend. We had coffee a couple of times after he taught the Introduction to Environment class."

"He must be quite a bit older than you if he's teaching at Berkeley."

"No, he's only a couple of years older. He's not a full professor. He's what's called a teaching assistant. Trace is working on his master's degree, and Berkeley has TA's teach a lot of the introductory classes. I think he'll really be a good professor."

"Olivia, you seem a little concerned about something. Does it have anything to do with this Trace guy?"

"Well, I can't put my finger on it, and since I haven't seen him for a couple of months, maybe I'm imagining it. I mentioned he teaches the intro class in Environmental Studies. Somehow he heard that there was this butterfly, it's called the Lotis Blue butterfly, and that it had been spotted on the Jefferson Lumber Company property.

Evidently it's on the Endangered Species List. When I talked to him on the phone he thought it would really be something if he could find it and be responsible for saving it. He told me it would help him when it came time for him to apply for admission to the doctorate program. He said that again today when we met."

"That doesn't seem unusual. Why the frown?"

"I don't remember Trace as being as intense as he was this afternoon. I mean he was really passionate about how important it was to save this butterfly, and then I noticed something I thought was strange. I remember that Trace had beautiful light brown eyes, and today I noticed that his eyes were light green."

"Maybe they were hazel and he wore brown contact lens sometimes and green ones sometimes. I read where a lot of people do that, and it's not just a female thing. The article I was reading said more and more men were wearing them for cosmetic effects."

"Yeah, you're probably right. I'm sure it's nothing. I thought I'd make spaghetti for dinner tonight, and it's been a long time since I had that special chocolate filling and frosting that grandma used to make for her yellow cakes, so I thought I'd make that too. I stopped and bought a cake mix and the frosting stuff on the way home. I thought the girls would like it."

"I don't think they'll like it. I know they will. Thanks, Olivia. I don't know what we'd do around here without you. You've been our lifesaver."

"Mom, now that you're feeling a little better, I need to see about getting a job. When I was in town I saw Bart Stevenson. I'm sure you remember him; he's the owner of the Red Cedar Tribune. He told me he'd heard I was back in town and asked how you were feeling. I told him you were making progress, and he said if I ever needed a job to give him a call. He said he was interested in getting a younger person's slant on what was happening locally. I think I'll give him a call."

"You could do a lot worse than Bart. He's a good man. I've known him for what seems like forever. We went to school together."

"Okay, I'm off to the kitchen. Do you need anything first?"

"No sweetie, not a thing. I'm going to watch TV for awhile and then I'll probably take a nap, so I can be fresh for the girls when they get home."

CHAPTER SEVEN

After she left home, Ruby drove to her job at the California Forestry Service office, parked her car, and walked in. The first person she saw was David Sanders. She gulped involuntarily, as he looked up and smiled at her. He walked over to her and said, "It's a little overdue, but I guess best wishes are in order on the occasion of your recent marriage. I hope he appreciates what a wonderful woman he's getting."

She struggled to keep calm and answered, "Yes, I'd like to think he does. What are you doing here? Are you the reason a meeting was called for this afternoon?"

"Yes. We've got a little issue that's come up in your district. Evidently there's been a spotting of a Lotis Blue butterfly. Don't know if you're aware of it, but it's on the Endangered Species List, and if the location of the sighting is correct, it might mean a whole lot of trouble for the Jefferson Lumber Company."

"I'm completely unfamiliar with it, but I imagine that would be a huge problem for them if it turns out to be true. I've heard they've also had a problem with an employee being diagnosed with cancer. There's a lot of talk around town he got cancer from exposure to formaldehyde at their plywood plant. Evidently it wasn't handled properly. "

"I don't know anything about that," David said. "I'm going to spend a little time telling your group about the Lotis Blue butterfly, and then I'm going out to where it's supposed to have been spotted. Your boss told me I could take one of his employees with me. I'd like you to join me," he said smiling at her with his dazzling million dollar smile she'd tried so hard to forget.

She was quiet for several moments and then said, "I'm not sure that's a good idea, David. I almost feel like we have a little unfinished business concerning our relationship, and I know George, that's my husband, wouldn't be happy about it. He's had some anger issues in the past, and I don't want to give him a reason to bring up those kinds of issues."

"I can understand that. If I were married to you, I wouldn't be very happy about my wife going out alone in the woods with her ex-lover, but I would like you to think about it. I need to give my talk now." He turned and walked away.

The whole time David was talking to her fellow Forestry Service employees, Ruby's mind was struggling. She remembered the good times with David, the fun they'd had, and the many nights they'd spent enjoying each other. She wondered if she'd been wrong to leave him. After all, a lot of people thought that his sibling, or in his case, his step-sibling, had inherited things she wasn't entitled to.

Ruby had just gotten tired of him constantly complaining about it, and one night when once again he'd brought it up, she told him she didn't want to be with someone who lived in the past. She knew theirs had been a strange relationship, and that she was young enough to be his daughter, but it hadn't mattered to her. She couldn't deny that she was still very physically attracted to David. She decided it wouldn't hurt to spend one last afternoon with David, and she'd make sure George never found out about it.

When David had finished talking to the employees about the Lotis Blue butterfly, she walked over to him and said, "I know I probably shouldn't do this, but I'd like to see this butterfly you were talking about. Why don't I meet you at the lumber company property in about half an hour?"

He looked down at her and gave her his killer grin which had never failed to make her heart skip a beat. "I'd like that, Ruby. I'd like that a lot. I was hoping I'd have a chance to see you and talk to you. Matter of fact I even brought a bottle of Stag's Leap wine which I remember was your favorite wine. Think of it as a wedding present from me to you. I'll be leaving in just a few minutes, and we can have a couple of hours to ourselves out at the property. Let me get you a map of where we'll be going. There's a copy machine over there. It'll just take a moment."

A few minutes later David walked out to the parking lot and got in his car. A half hour later Ruby walked out and got into her car. Neither one of them saw George's car parked behind a nearby dumpster.

CHAPTER EIGHT

"Liz, that dinner was fabulous. I could tell that the cottage guests liked it every bit as much as I did. I've never had pork cooked like that. Was it hard to fix?"

"No. It's embarrassingly easy. I just rub it down with a barbecue seasoning salt, sear it in a frying pan on all sides in a little oil and then exactly twenty-three minutes before I want it to be ready, I stick it in the oven. How easy is that?"

"Easy, but what was that sauce? I've never had anything like it."

"It's called a chipotle raspberry sauce. Actually I got the recipe from a man who lives in Santa Fe. His name is Erick and he was staying in one of the cottages. He's the one who also told me he served that sauce with the pork. I think it goes with it perfectly."

"Me too, and I gotta tell you that dessert was delicious. You know I'm an ice cream freak, so that was a no brainer for me. I especially liked that raspberry balsamic sauce that was drizzled over it. I've never had anything like that before. Yeah, that was a real hit."

"The recipe originally called for pistachio ice cream along with the strawberry and chocolate, but I prefer the green tea ice cream. Glad you liked it. I've got a couple more things to do in the kitchen, and then I'll join you downstairs."

"See you in a few minutes," he said as he walked towards the stairs leading to the lower level of the lodge. Just before they'd gotten married, they'd remodeled a downstairs storeroom next to Liz's living quarters and made it into a home office and a den for Roger. Floor to ceiling windows had been installed, so Roger could look out at the Pacific Ocean when he was working, a view he never tired of.

"Liz," he said a moment later walking back up the stairs, "your phone was ringing when I got downstairs, so I answered it. It's Seth." He handed the phone to her. She grimaced as she took it from him.

"Hello, Seth. How are you?" she asked. Seth Williams was the Red Cedar Chief of Police, and Liz would be the first to admit she had a love/hate relationship with him. On one hand she couldn't believe that voters kept re-electing the obese, bumbling, insensitive man to the position he held. Yet, on the other hand, there was something about him that was childishly appealing. There was no love/hate relationship on Seth's part. He clearly idolized Liz, a fact that hadn't escaped Roger's attention. Liz was aware that Roger hadn't gone back downstairs.

"I'm fine, Liz, jes' fine. I was jes' fixin' to get in bed, 'cuz I was so busy givin' out speedin' tickets today that I'm all tuckered out. Anyway, jes' got a call from George Myers. Ya' know him?"

"No, Seth, I can't say that I do."

"Well, he was all cryin' and sayin' his wife, Ruby, hadn't come home yet and could I do somethin' about it, like find her. Yeah, like I could find her at this hour of the night. Been my experience if'n a woman or man don't want to be found 'bout this time a night, ain't no way I can find 'em. He said sometimes she goes to that bar on the other side of town, the Last Chance Saloon, with a friend after work, so he wasn't too concerned when she was late comin' home from work. He called the bar a little while ago, and they tol' him she weren't never there tonight. Says he's worried somethin' mighta' happened to her. I tol' him if she ain't home by tomorrow mornin' we'll start lookin' for her. Reason I'm callin' you is to ask you to keep a heads up for her, ya' bein' the one everybody seems to talk to all the time."

"I'll keep my eyes and ears open, and if I see or hear something I'll let you know, but since I've never met her, rather doubt that will happen. Talk to you soon, Seth. Good night."

"Nite purty lady. Ya' tell that Roger he's one lucky dog."

"Thanks." She ended the call and saw Roger looking at her and shaking his head. "What?" she asked.

"I overheard what that joke of a police chief said, along with everything else. I really don't like another man talking like that to my wife."

"Oh, Roger, that's just Seth. He's really harmless."

"Okay, I'll let it go. That name, Ruby, rings a bell with me. Let me think about it while you're finishing up in the kitchen. I can't quite pull the trigger on..."

He was interrupted by Liz's phone. "Sorry, Roger, I better take this. It's Gertie. I wonder why she's calling at this time of night."

"Hi, Gertie. How are you?"

"I'm fine, honey. Jes' wondered if my step-brother made it to dinner at the lodge tonight?"

"No. He wasn't here. I thought you said he wasn't coming for dinner, so I wasn't expecting him."

"Well, even though him and me had words at lunch, thought he'd probably stop by here for some dinner, but he didn't. Do ya' know if he's in his cottage?"

"No, I haven't been out since dinner. If you're concerned, Roger and I can walk down there and see."

"I don't want ya' to do that. He's probably sound asleep by now. Guess I'm just feelin' a little guilty 'bout that set-to we had in the kitchen at lunch. Don't worry none about it. I'll talk to him tomorrow. I'm sure he'll come here fer breakfast. I'll call ya' after we talk."

"Must be a night for missing persons. I just talked to Seth. Do you happen to know a woman named Ruby?" Liz asked.

"Why?"

"Well, evidently her husband called, and she hasn't come home tonight. Seth seemed to think it wasn't that uncommon and insinuated that it was probably a male-female thing."

There was a long silence on the other end of the phone. Finally Gertie spoke. "Liz, honey, I don't wanna think what I'm thinkin'. When Ruby moved here two years ago, she came to the diner and introduced herself. She and my step-brother, David Sanders, had been romantically involved when she was livin' in Sacramento, but she'd left him 'cuz he was always jawin' 'bout how he shoulda got his dad's money, not my momma and then me. I like her."

"Gertie, I honestly don't know what to say. I saw your step-brother today when I walked into the kitchen at lunch time to see if you were all right, but to my knowledge I've never met her. I'm a little reluctant to go down to his cabin with this information. I guess what happens, if anything, between consenting adults is their business and not mine."

"Honey, I wish it were that easy. Here's the thing. Ruby married George Myers after she broke up with David and moved here from Sacramento. George works out at the Jefferson Lumber Company. Guy's got a real temper. When he was a teen he was always gettin' in fights. Matter of fact he spent a little time in jail for beatin' a guy up real bad when he found him in bed with his girlfriend. Ruby comes in from time to time, and she tol' me he'd been gettin' some anger counselin' and it was workin'. Said that was why she married him. Liz, I got a real bad feelin' 'bout this. If George thinks Ruby and

David are together, he's got such a bad temper he could kill him."

"What do you want me to do, Gertie?"

"Let's see what happens in the mornin'. I'm gonna think good thoughts about it. Y'all get some sleep. I'll talk to ya' tomorrow."

"Good night, Gertie, and thanks for the call."

When she'd ended the call she turned to Roger. "Did you hear that conversation?"

"Yes, and I agree with Gertie. I don't think it sounds very good. You stay here. I'm going to walk down to the cottage where David's staying. I remember you mentioned at lunch that he was staying in number one. I just want to see if there's a car next to it. I won't knock or anything. Be back in a couple of minutes. I'd take Brandy Boy with me, but we both know how worthless he is. I'll take Winston." He turned to Winston. "Come on, boy." A moment later they walked out the door.

When they returned Roger had a worried look on his face. "There's no car parked next to the cottage, and no lights are on in the cottage. It didn't appear that anyone was there. I don't know what to make of that."

"Do you think I should call Gertie?"

"No, the only thing it would do is cause her more worry. Let's see what happens in the morning. Fortunately I don't have anything at the office until tomorrow afternoon. I've got to go into San Francisco for a partnership meeting at the firm. Winston took care of business during our walk, so he's fine." He turned off the lights, and he and Liz walked down the stairs to their living quarters.

When he got to the bottom of the stairs he hit his forehead with the palm of his hand. "Now I remember where I heard the names Ruby and George. When I had the meeting with Lewis Jefferson today he mentioned that for the first time in a long time he didn't seem to have any employee problems. He said occasionally a guy named George Myers used to be a problem. Got drunk and missed work from time to time. Said he got into fights a lot, but he'd fallen in love with a woman named Ruby and after getting some anger counseling, he seemed to have left those days behind him. Pretty much a coincidence, don't you think? I mean Lewis tells me about this guy, and Seth calls you about him, and then Gertie mentions him."

"Well, this seems to be the day for them. First the blue butterfly and now this one. Hopefully, Ruby will be home in the morning, and David will show up at Gertie's Diner for breakfast. I thought he was attractive, so maybe he met up with someone, and they decided to spend a little time together."

"I really don't like to hear that you find another man attractive. What have I become, chopped liver?"

"I guess I didn't phrase that very well. What I meant was that someone else might find him attractive, but I still think you're the most attractive man in the world."

"Nice recovery, Liz," he said grinning.

Liz didn't tell Roger that she felt the niggle, that inner knowing she occasionally got when something wasn't quite right. And the niggle had never been wrong.

CHAPTER NINE

Brad Cassidy stared at the IV bag holding the chemotherapy chemical that was slowly dripping into his arm. Although he became terribly ill after each treatment, his doctor told him he had to have the chemotherapy treatment. He said if it worked there was a good chance his cancer would go into remission. If his cancer did go into remission, it would be worth losing his hair and being so weak at times it was all he could do to get out of bed. Days went by when he could barely function, and he felt like a shell of the man he had once been.

His doctor had also been very clear he couldn't ever go back to work at the plywood plant, and there was a very good chance he would never be able to work again. Brad worried about what the loss of income would mean to his wife and his two little children, much less his death, if it came to that.

I guess I was just at the wrong place at the wrong time. I thought when I left Afghanistan that nothin' could be worse than what I saw over there. I was wrong. My life has become far worse. The doctor says I have a form of myeloid leukemia that was probably caused by bein' exposed to formaldehyde for so many years at the plywood plant. He thinks I got a good chance of gettin' some type of a settlement from Jefferson and said he'd testify if I sued 'em. Good thinkin' on his part, because the letter I wrote to Lewis Jefferson sure didn't get me nowhere. If I die what are Becky and the kids supposed to live on? And if I can't work, what are they supposed to live on? And if I did sue Jefferson, what would happen to

Jimmy and my other friends out at the plant? The way the lumber industry's been goin' they'd probably all be out of work if I won a large settlement. Heard some talk that Jefferson's barely able to keep the plant open as it is. I don't want to be the one responsible for them not havin' any money and their families goin' through what we're goin' through.

I don't know how much longer we can hang on. I've maxed out all of our credit cards, my car's been repossessed, and the house is in foreclosure. Some husband and father I am. I can't even take care of my family.

Becky had told him she'd stick by him no matter what and so she had, but it killed him to see her working two jobs to support the family. Week by week he saw her aging before his very eyes trying to do everything. Her mother had been great about keeping the kids when Brad was just too exhausted or in too much pain to even get out of bed, much less try and babysit two rambunctious little boys that were too young to be in school.

The pain and worrying about his young family had taken its toll on Brad. His future looked bleak, and his mounting anger began to focus on the president of Jefferson Lumber Company, Lewis Jefferson.

Livin' in that fancy house of his and driving that big Cadillac SUV, he sure don't know what it's like for someone like me. I hate him. Least he could do is give me somethin' to live on, somethin' for Becky and the kids. Jimmy tol' me he goes out to where the crew's been loggin' every day to make sure the work is gettin' done on schedule. Jimmy said somethin' about a blue butterfly, and that it might cause some problems fer the company. Sure would like to find it and make some problems for mister big shot Jefferson. Maybe he'd understand what I'm goin' thru if he had to stop loggin' because of it. Might not be able to afford his fancy car and house anymore.

While Brad was reclining in the chair waiting for the IV drip to finish, a plan began to form in his mind, a way that he might be able to get what he felt was owed him because Lewis Jefferson hadn't made sure that his manager at the plywood plant followed the required industry safety standards when working with formaldehyde.

CHAPTER TEN

"Roger, we really slept in. I can't believe it's almost 8:00. Good thing you don't have any early appointments with clients this morning," Liz said as she leaped out of bed and headed for the shower. "Mind if I go first?"

"No, like I told you last night, my morning is free, so if we had to pick a day to oversleep, this is a good one to do it. Take your time. I'll make us some coffee and let Winston out."

A few minutes later she walked out of the bathroom in her favorite white terrycloth bathrobe, a towel wrapped around her wet hair. "I can't wake up. I really need coffee this morning, thanks," she said as she took the cup he handed her. "If you're okay with it, I'll finish up in the bathroom, and then it's all yours."

"No problem. I'll watch the news and see what's happening in the world. If it's like most days, I'll probably turn it off after a couple of minutes, because I'm so disgusted by what's in the news these days." A few minutes later he poked his head into the bathroom and said, "Liz, your phone's ringing. Want me to get it?"

"Please. Tell whoever it is I'll be with them in a minute."

When she walked out of the bathroom and took the phone from Roger, she mouthed the words "Who is it?"

Roger covered the phone and said, "Seth, and he doesn't sound like himself."

"Good morning, Seth. How are you?"

"Not good, Liz, ain't good at all."

"What's the problem>"

Seth sighed and said, "Got me a murder on my hands and much as I hate to ask, need your help."

Liz sat down on the bed and asked, "Is it anyone I know?"

"Don't know, but you sure know his step-sister, cuz it's Gertie's step-brother who done gone and got hisself shot and killed."

"Oh no, poor Gertie! How's she taking it?"

"Here's the thing. She don't know 'bout it yet, leastways I don't think she does. See, I gotta stay here with the body. You remember Wes, the coroner. Well I called him and 'tol him to bring the meat wagon, cuz I got's him a fresh dead body. He's on his way, so I can't leave. That's why I need yer' help. You bein' such a good friend of Gertie's, I was thinkin' maybe you could go get her and bring her out here. Gotta have next of kin identify the body. Don't know if he's got a wife or kids, but a sister'll do even if she is a step-sister."

"Where is here?"

"There's a section of land owned by the Jefferson Lumber Company that's in the city limits of Red Cedar out on the east side of town. That's where the body was found, so it's in my jurisdiction," Seth said importantly.

"Who found the body?" Liz asked.

"Well, this is kinda strange. I had a 'nonymous call from some woman 'bout an hour ago tellin' me that David Sanders had been shot and killed. She tol' me where the body was, so yours truly's the one who found him. She wouldn't give me her name or where she was callin' from. Don't know nuthin' more than that. I gotta go Liz, I hear a lot of loud sounds, and I think some lumbermen are gettin' ready to cut down some nearby trees. Gotta stop 'em. This here location is now an official crime scene. Can ya' get Gertie and bring her out here fer me?"

"Yes," Liz sighed. "I'll go over to the diner now and tell her. I'll take Roger with me, and we'll be out there as soon as we can. Tell me specifically where you are." She listened to his directions and ended the call. "Roger, I assume you heard that."

"Yes. I need to call my client, Lewis Jefferson. He should be notified, because it happened on his property. Since we're both going to go to the diner, why don't you drive, and I'll call him on the way over there to save time? I really don't want Gertie to hear this from someone else and who knows who that oafish police chief might call. He's a legend only in his own mind. I still can't figure out how he gets elected every time he runs for police chief."

Minutes later they were dressed and on their way. When Roger had finished talking to Lewis he said, "Lewis is going to meet us out at his property. I'm not looking forward to you having to tell Gertie about her step-brother. Having that argument with him yesterday sure doesn't help the situation."

"Yes, I'm sure she's going to really regret they had bitter words the last time she saw him."

"Liz, that's not quite what I meant. From what Seth was saying, I got the idea that he'd been murdered. Having an argument that was heard by a number of people probably on the same day he was murdered doesn't make it look very good for Gertie."

Liz looked over at him wide-eyed and said, "You've got to be kidding. Gertie doesn't have a mean bone in her body. You can't possibly think anyone would even suggest she would do something like that."

"I couldn't agree more with you, but everyone may not share our feelings. Look, there's an empty parking spot right in front of her diner. Why don't you pull in there?"

They walked into the diner and were greeted by Gertie. "Two days in a row? You may jes' become my two most favorite customers. Course handsome here's already my favorite tenant now that he's rentin' that office next door."

"Gertie," Liz said somberly, "could we go into your office? We have some bad news and need to talk to you privately."

She looked from Liz to Roger and said, "It's about David, ain't it? Somethin's happened to him. I felt it in my bones all night."

Liz put her arm around Gertie and led her into her office, while Roger spoke to one of the waitresses he knew from his frequent lunches at Gertie's. He told her Gertie would be leaving for the day and to call him if there was a problem. Roger jotted down his cell phone number, gave it to her, and then walked into Gertie's office.

"Liz, I know George Myers had somethin' to do with David's death. Has Seth talked to him?" he heard Gertie say.

Roger realized Liz had already told Gertie about David's death, and said, "Gertie, I am so sorry. We'll help Seth find out who did this, but speaking as an attorney who specializes in criminal defense work, I don't want you saying anything to Seth or anyone else about the murder without me being present."

"That's about the silliest thing I ever heard. Seth and me go way back. Course I'll talk to him and tell him everything he wants to know."

"Gertie, I don't quite know how to tell you this, so I guess I'll just say it straight out. You and David had an argument yesterday. Almost everyone who was in the diner heard it. As lazy and as bad a police chief as Seth is, he's going to look for the low lying fruit when he's trying to solve this case. What I'm saying is you could be considered a suspect, and since Seth is a lot more worried about giving out tickets to speeders than anything else, he might not spend the time necessary to find out who murdered your step-brother. He might prefer to blame it on someone more convenient..."

Gertie interrupted him, "Roger, are you sayin' what I think you're sayin'? That I could be considered a suspect in my own step-brother's murder? That's jes' plain crazy. Mark my words. What that stupid fat police chief oughta be doin' is talkin' to George Myers."

"Seth asked me to take you to where the murder occurred and have you identify David's body," Liz said. "Let's get it over with, and then we'll go to the lodge. You may not realize it, but right now you're probably in shock. You need some time to get over it. Staying out at the lodge with me for a few hours will be good for you. Roger, I know you have a meeting later this afternoon, so you can get your car when I take Gertie to the lodge and then you can come back here and check on things at the diner before you go to your office. Gertie, let's leave through the kitchen door."

"I told Suzie to tell the staff you had a family emergency and had to leave for the day," Roger said, "so you don't need to say anything to them. Follow me."

The three of them walked out the back door of the diner and got into Liz's van. Tears had started streaming down Gertie's face. "I can't believe I yelled at my step-brother the last time I saw him. I'll never forgive myself for the things I said. Maybe if I hadn't said those things, he'd still be alive."

"Gertie, I was afraid you'd feel that way. What happened was a family argument, and those are pretty common occurrences. You had no way of knowing what was going to happen. It's going to be hard enough to get over his death. Don't make it any worse by blaming yourself," Roger said. Gertie looked out the window and continued to sob as they drove towards the east side of town where the Jefferson Lumber Company property was located.

CHAPTER ELEVEN

"The Jefferson Lumber property is up here on the right," Roger said to Liz who was driving her van.

"I've never been down this gravel side road before. The forest is really dense here," Liz said. "It comes right up to both sides of the road. It's so dark you can barely see twenty feet back into it."

"It's interesting," Roger said. "I drove down this road once when I found out that Jefferson Lumber Company was going to be my client. Evidently years ago all of this land was a national forest, and then the government decided to sell a portion of it. Lewis Jefferson's grandfather bought the property, and it's been in the family ever since. When I called him a few minutes ago he told me there's a parking lot about a half a mile down the road from where we turned off the main highway. He said the boundary line separating the Jefferson Lumber Company property from the U.S. Forest Service land starts at the parking lot. He also said the lot usually has cars in it because people go on day hikes on trails maintained by the Forest Service, and some of his employees use the lot too. He told me to take the trail on the right, and it should lead to the place where we're to meet Seth."

"Roger, look over there at that building in that large cleared out open space. It's an art gallery, for crying out loud. Guess whoever owns it figures he or she will get some business from the people who come out here to go hiking."

Gertie cleared her throat and said, "That's Joan Markham's gallery. Been here a long time. Specializes in paintings of people set in Northern California scenes. Sends a lot of her work to some gallery down in San Francisco. Hear she's purty good, but I don't really know nothin' 'bout what's good and what's not when it comes to art."

"I've been looking for some artwork to put in the lodge that's been done by a local artist. I'll have to pay her a visit. Smart of her to put her gallery directly across the road from the parking lot. I imagine a lot of people stop at her gallery after a hike on some of the local trails." She slowed the van down and turned right into the parking lot.

Liz, Roger, and Gertie got out of the van after Liz parked in the parking lot, and the three of them started walking down the path on the right that led into the forest and the area Seth had described to Liz. Roger held Gertie's arm, so she wouldn't stumble on the uneven ground, since she was wearing her customary five inch high stiletto heels. They hadn't gone far when they saw Wes, the coroner, and Seth standing next to a sheet on the ground covering what appeared to be a body. Standing a short distance away from them were several lumberjacks and a man Liz assumed was Lewis Jefferson.

"Gertie, sorry 'bout your loss. Need ya' to take a look-see under the sheet and tell me if'n that's your step-brother, then I wanna talk to ya'," Seth said.

Supported by Roger, she hesitantly walked over to where the body was lying on the ground. Gertie knelt down and gingerly lifted up a corner of the sheet. She gasped, hastily replaced the sheet, and said with her voice shaking, "Yes, that's, that's David. I can't believe it. Who coulda done this?" She backed away from the body and looked at Seth.

She pointed her finger at him and said, "Ya' need to talk to George Myers. He hated my brother, because David and his wife lived together when they was in Sacramento. I know he's the one who did it."

"Well, Gertie, don't know nothin' 'bout that, but lotta people tol' me you and yer' step-brother had a real dustup yesterday at yer' diner. What about that?"

Roger stepped between them and said, "Seth, I'm representing Gertie, and she has no comment. If you have any further questions for her, you'll have to go through me."

"Whatcha talkin' 'bout Roger? All I'm doin' is jes' tryin' to find out 'bout some mean words said to a man who was murdered later in the day." From the tone of his voice there was no doubt he was convinced Gertie was the murderer.

"You heard what I said. I want to talk to Lewis for a moment, but first I'm going to escort Gertie to the van. I'll be right back."

"Liz, need to talk to ya'," Seth said. "Don't know what bee's gotten into his bonnet. Anyway, this one looks like it's gonna be a tough one, him bein' from outta town and all. You've gotten lucky before and helped me solve a case or two. Probably could use yer' help on this one. Deputy's on his way. We're gonna look for the weapon, and Wes is gonna take the body in his meat wagon. I'll talk to you later."

After taking Gertie back to the van, Roger walked over to where Lewis Jefferson was standing with several of his lumberjack employees. "Roger, this is a mess. Remember when I told you about that blue butterfly thing. Well, this is where it was spotted. I wanted to get this land cleared before some radical enviro activist got a cease and desist order from a friendly judge. Now the police chief says we have to halt all work on this section, because it's an active crime scene. I can't believe it. I think I'm snake bit with this section of land, plus I'm not looking forward to seeing Jefferson Lumber in the media as being the scene of a murder. If it gets out that some endangered species butterfly was also sighted here, all the enviro wackos in Northern California will be breathing down my neck. What can I do about it?"

"I'm going to give you the same advice I gave Gertie a little while ago. I'm your attorney and simply say that any and all questions should be directed to me. Tell them you have no comment. Hopefully this won't be a crime scene for too long, and you can continue to harvest the timber on this land before some enviro gets a court order."

"Well, that will have to do for now, I guess. That fat police chief wants to talk to my men who were in the area yesterday and find out if any of them know anything. From what they're telling me, none of them saw anything."

"All right. All we can do now is keep our fingers crossed. Let me know when Seth says it's okay for your men to resume work. One last thing. Are these all the men who were here yesterday?" Roger asked.

Lewis walked over to where his men were standing and talked to them for a moment. He came back to Roger and said, "Evidently Mark Bailey took a vacation day today. Something about some dental work he had to get done. His foreman expects him back tomorrow. Do you want me to have him call you?"

"Yes, please."

"One more thing, Roger. I couldn't help but overhear that woman tell the police chief he needed to talk to George Myers. I think I mentioned him to you when we met yesterday. He didn't show up for work today. Do you know anything about him?"

"No, but anything that's out of the ordinary probably needs to be looked into. I'll tell my wife."

Lewis looked confused. "I may be missing something here, Roger, but I don't understand why you need to tell your wife something like that."

"I understand your confusion, Lewis. Liz seems to have a sixth sense when it comes to solving murders. She's been able to solve several local murder cases, and I'm sure she'll be helping with this one. Even though she's not formally trained, she's been very successful in the past."

"Glad it's your wife and not mine. I don't think I'd like my wife to be involved in anything like this. I have some meetings scheduled for this morning, so I need to take off. Call me if you hear anything," Lewis said as he walked towards his SUV.

"Same for you," Roger said. He walked over to where Seth and Liz were talking. "Liz, are you about ready to go? I'd like to take Gertie back to the lodge. This has to be very hard for her."

"Yes." She turned to Seth and said, "I'll call you later. I'd like to know if you find the murder weapon." She walked to the van where Gertie sat stony-faced looking away from where her step-brother's body was being lifted into the coroner's van.

CHAPTER TWELVE

After they'd made sure Gertie was comfortable, and Roger had left to tell the staff at the diner what had happened, Liz made a list of things she thought needed to be done. She walked into the great room where Gertie was looking out the window, apparently deep in thought.

"Gertie, David had a uniform on when I saw him at the diner yesterday. You told me he had something to do with the Forestry Service. Who exactly did he work for?"

"Worked for the California Forestry Service. Oh my gosh, I need to call their local office here in Red Cedar. He was working with them on that blue butterfly thing. They need to know he's...dead."

"I'll call them for you. You just sit here and rest."

Liz returned a few moments later. "Gertie I called the office, and they were shocked and saddened. Evidently your step-brother was very well liked. The manager of the office asked if there was anything he could do, and I told him no, and then he said something I think is kind of odd. He said he thought it was very strange that both David and another woman that works there hadn't shown up for work today. He went on to say David's death certainly explained why David wasn't there, but he wondered where the woman was since she hadn't asked for the day off or called in sick."

Gertie was quiet for several minutes and then said, "Liz, do you remember when I tol' you about Ruby, the woman David lived with in Sacramento? 'Member I tol' you how she left David and moved to Red Cedar, and about six months ago she married George Myers? She works for the Forestry Service. That's how they met. Do you suppose that's the woman who didn't show up for work today?"

"I have no idea. I'll call the manager back and ask him. I also need to find out if he knows what David was doing out on the Jefferson Lumber Company property. I wonder if it had something to do with the blue butterfly. I'll be back in a few minutes. Can I get you anything?"

"No thanks, honey, I jes' appreciate everything yer' doin' fer me. I don't think David was ever at yer' cottage, but I probably better see if he stopped in and left some stuff. I also need to call the Forestry Service in Sacramento and tell 'em. Ya' know David and I didn't have no other relatives. He never married and never had no kids. I probably better get someone to clear out his apartment in Sacramento. Don't know if he had a Will."

"I'll take care of all of that. The only thing you need to do is take care of yourself," Liz said, making more notes. "I'll be in the other room making some calls." She walked into her office and closed the door. She didn't know what she was going to learn from the calls she was about to make, but whatever it was, she preferred to not have Gertie overhear her conversations.

"Hello, this is the Sacramento office of the California Forestry Service. How may I direct your call?" the young woman asked.

"My name is Liz Langley, and I'd like to speak with the person in charge of your office. It's a personal matter. Thank you."

"That would be Mitch Stevenson. Just a moment please, and I'll connect you."

A few minutes went by and then a deep male voice said, "This is Mitch Stevenson. I understand what you want to talk to me about is a personal matter. How may I help you?"

"Thank you for taking my call, Mr. Stevenson. I'm sorry to tell you this, but one of your employees, David Sanders, was murdered late yesterday. His step-sister is with me, and she asked that I call your office."

"Oh no! That's horrible! I can't believe it. What happened?"

Liz relayed what she knew and then said, "Can you recommend someone who might be able to clean out his apartment? His step-sister is his only living relative, but she owns a diner here in Red Cedar and can't take the time off to do it."

"Of course. I'll call you back with a name. Actually, my wife and I have a cleaning lady we've used for years. She's very trustworthy, and I think she could use the extra work."

"That would be wonderful. I understand David never married and didn't have any children. I wonder if there's a Will or the name of an attorney somewhere in his residence."

"David lived in an apartment, and I'm sure the apartment manager would have a key. The name of the apartment is probably in David's personnel records. I'll find out the details and ask Ellie, that's my cleaning lady, if she'd be willing to do it. I'm sure she would, so plan on me calling you once she's had a chance to go out there. May I have your phone number?"

"Of course." Liz gave it to him, thanked him, and then said, "I have a question about something that's bothering me. I understand at one time David was romantically involved with a woman who worked in your office a couple of years ago. I don't know what her maiden name was, but her first name is Ruby. Does that ring a bell with you?"

It was very quiet on the other end of the phone, and then Mitch began to speak. "That was a rather delicate situation. We have an office policy that employees are not supposed to be romantically involved. Ruby and David were both very good employees, and I overlooked the situation once it came to my attention. For whatever reason, they ended the relationship and shortly thereafter, Ruby requested a transfer. There was an opening in Red Cedar, and she transferred there. I had misgivings about sending David to that office yesterday knowing she worked there, but I figured they were adults, and their relationship had ended two years ago. I sincerely hope their past relationship didn't have anything to do with his death."

"I have no idea, however I do have one more question, if you don't mind. David mentioned something about a blue butterfly to his step-sister, and that was apparently the reason he came to Red Cedar. Can you tell me anything about that?"

"Yes. I sent David there because our department received a letter along with a photograph that a Lotis Blue butterfly, which is on the Endangered Species List, had been spotted in a forest on the Jefferson Lumber Company's land. I asked him to see what he could find out. Things like this are very difficult for us because we often get caught in the middle of disputes between big business and environmentalists. If a Lotis Blue butterfly had been sighted, and if an environmentalist was able to get a cease and desist order from a judge, it could result in the lumber company having to stop all timber harvesting activities for often what becomes a prolonged period of time or possibly forever. I wanted David to determine if the reported butterfly sighting was valid."

"Do you know if he found out anything?"

"No, I talked to the manager of our Red Cedar office late yesterday, and he mentioned David had spoken to his employees yesterday afternoon about the possible sighting, and then he left the office to go out to the site."

"Do you know if anyone went with him?"

"No. If someone did the manager didn't mention it to me."

"I can't thank you enough for your help. Please give my phone number to Ellie and tell her I look forward to hearing what she's found out. I imagine this will involve several days of work on her part. I'm sure David's step-sister will want his personal possessions donated to non-profit organizations, and she will want Ellie to oversee that as well. I'll wait for her call. Again, thanks."

Liz called the local Red Cedar forestry office back and asked to speak with the manager. "I'm sorry to bother you again. I just got off the phone with Mitch Stevenson over at the Sacramento office where David Sanders worked. He mentioned he had spoken with you late yesterday, and that David was going to the area where a Lotis Blue butterfly had allegedly been sighted. Do you know if anyone else from your office went with him?"

"I don't think so. Everyone was here in the late afternoon, oh, everyone except Ruby Myers. She told me she had some personal business she had to attend to and needed to take the rest of the afternoon off. I think that accounts for everyone."

"Thanks. So you don't know whether or not David was able to spot a Lotis Blue butterfly."

"No, I don't. I probably better talk to Mitch and see if he wants to send someone else over here or if one of my staff should go out there and see if they can spot the butterfly. I know he wants to get some resolution on this before all heck breaks loose."

"Yes, that's pretty much what he told me. Again, thanks. I really appreciate your help."

Liz walked down the hall to Bertha's office, knocked, and opened the door. "Bertha, I have some bad news. David Sanders, Gertie's step-brother, was murdered late yesterday."

"Oh, no!" she said, rising out of her chair and gripping the edge of her desk. "That's terrible. Poor Gertie. How's she doing?"

"She's here at the lodge. She wanted to go back to the diner, but Roger was very firm in insisting she stay here and rest today. I don't think her step-brother ever came to cottage number one, but on the off chance he did, would you have someone check and see if there's anything of his in there? Thanks."

"Of course. I'll see to it immediately. What else can I do?"

"I can't think of anything at the moment. I need to get ready for tonight. I'll let you know if I hear anything."

"Liz, is Seth going to be in charge of this case?"

"It's in his jurisdiction, so technically, yes."

"Reading between the lines, I'm getting the impression that you're going to be involved in it, and Roger probably will be as well. Am I right?"

"Yes, I suppose your impression is correct. See you later."

CHAPTER THIRTEEN

"Is there anything I can do for you?" Liz asked Gertie.

Gertie turned away from where she'd been idly looking at the ocean and said, "No, honey. You and Roger have been so good to me. Thank you. I'm gonna call Suzie down at the diner, and she can pick me up. I know it's gettin' near time fer ya' to feed yer' guests, and ya' got better things to do than wait on me hand and foot. Is Roger gonna be here soon? I'd like to thank him for helpin' me today."

"No, he had to go into San Francisco for a partner's meeting. He told me he was having dinner with a couple of them, and he'd drive home after that. Let me know when Suzie gets here. I need to tell Gina what to do in order to get ready for dinner tonight."

"How's she workin' out? I know you were purty sorry to lose Emily when she went to that fancy schmancy culinary school in San Francisco. Gina gonna be able to fill her shoes?"

"Yes, she's been great. Actually, Emily was the one who recommended her, and I'm glad she did. That knock on the door you hear is probably her." Liz walked over and greeted Gina. "Gina, you know Gertie. She's spending a little time with me."

Gina greeted Gertie, turned to Liz and asked, "What would you like me to get started on?"

"We're having catfish primavera with fettucine and a large tossed salad. I'd like you to prep the vegetables. The recipe's on the counter in the kitchen. You can get started while I answer this call."

She walked over to her phone and answered it. "This is Liz Langley." She listened for a minute and said, "Seth, start over. What's the problem?" Out of the corner of her eye she noticed that Gertie was sitting very still, trying to hear what Seth had to say. "Seth, I need to take this call in my office. Hold on for a moment." She walked into her office and closed the door, not sure what Seth was going to tell her, but not wanting Gertie to hear the conversation.

"Had my deputy trace that 'noymous call I got from a woman this mornin' tellin' me 'bout David bein' dead. Traced it to a number in Pleasantville."

"I've never heard of Pleasantville. Where is it?" Liz asked.

"It's 'bout twenty miles from here. Kinda small, like don't blink or ya' gonna miss it when ya' go thru it. Anyway, that telephone number belongs to a woman named Joyce Samuels. Here's where it gets interestin'. That guy George Myers I tol' you 'bout last night who kept callin' concernin' his missin' wife, well, he called a coupla more times today. I finally took his call, and he tol' me he'd driven over to Pleasantville to his mother-in-law's house to look-see if his wife was there, since he ain't findin' her anywhere else. Said he saw Ruby's car in the driveway, but nobody answered the door when he rang the bell. Here's the kicker. Turns out the phone number we got the call from 'bout Gertie's step-brother is registered to George Myers' mother-in-law. Didn't tell George 'bout it. Wanted to run it by ya'."

"Seth, do you think Ruby was the one who called you about David's death? Maybe she was at her mother's home and called you from there."

"Dunno, but it sure is a heck of a coincidence."

Yeah and I know what Roger thinks about those, and I have to agree, that's quite a coincidence.

"What are you planning on doing with the information?" Liz asked.

"Well, Liz, here's the thing. I gots me a lot of reports to fill out tomorrow 'bout this murder and all. Wonderin' if you could go over there and talk to the mother and Ruby, if she's there. Figure bein' women, they'd probably talk to ya' a little easier than they would to a police chief," Seth said in a voice filled with self-importance. "You know, lots of people are skeered to talk to people in uniforms."

Right. You just don't want to do this, and you're trying to pass it off to me, Liz thought.

"I can't do it today, Seth. It's almost time for my nightly dinner for the cottage guests, but I could do it in the morning." Liz admitted to herself she was curious what the two women would have to say.

"Great. Call me after ya' finish and lemme know what ya' find out. Here's her address, course being a little town like that ya' won't have any problem findin' it." He gave her the address, and she ended the call.

CHAPTER FOURTEEN

Liz held the front door of the lodge open as the last guest started to leave after dinner. "Honestly, Mrs. Langley, that was the best pasta I've ever had, and it had to be healthy since it was made with fish. I loved it. Would you mind giving me the recipe?" the attractive woman asked.

"Of course not. I'll have my manager copy it and leave it at the front desk at the spa for you. I'm glad you liked it."

"I've been here three times, and I've never had a bad meal. It's one of the reasons I keep coming back and telling all of my friends about your spa. I always feel so good after I've been here. I have to leave tomorrow afternoon, but I'll be back in a few months."

"Great. I'll look forward to seeing you again," Liz said, closing the door. She spent the next half hour helping Gina finish cleaning up the kitchen. "Gina, you've been here long enough. Go home, and I'll see you tomorrow afternoon. Thanks for everything. I'm really happy Emily referred you to me."

"So am I, Mrs. Langley. I love working here."

"Well," Liz said with a twinkle in her eye, "I'm glad you do, but if you're serious about staying, it's time to start calling me Liz instead of Mrs. Langley."

"Yes, Liz," Gina said grinning as she took her coat from the coat hook on the wall. "See you tomorrow."

Liz was letting Winston in when she saw the lights on Roger's car coming up the lane. She walked over to his car and said, "Hey handsome, if you don't have a place to stay tonight, how about bunking down here?"

"Think I'll take you up on that, pretty lady. I'm easy," he said as he got out of his car and put his arm around her. The three of them, Winston, Liz, and Roger, walked back into the lodge. She looked out one of the large floor to ceiling windows and said, "Look at the lights out on the ocean. Must be a cruise ship. It's beautiful."

"Whenever I look out that window or the ones from down below, I can't believe how different it is each time. One time I'll see an eagle and another time a pod of whales. Now I know why you bought this property. It's really special."

"I know. I feel so lucky, but this has been a long day, and I'm really tired."

"How's Gertie doing? Is she here or did she go home?"

"Suzie picked her up and took her home. I got a call from Seth. Remember when he called last night about the missing woman?" She told Roger about the conversation she'd had with Seth.

Roger walked into the bathroom, and returned a moment later holding his toothbrush. "Liz, I've been thinking. I'm a little concerned about you going to that woman's house tomorrow. What if this Ruby woman murdered David? They have a history, and who knows what took place? Maybe she wanted to get back at him for something, perhaps some sort of revenge."

"I don't think I'll be in any danger. I'm not getting the niggle that's usually present at the first sign of trouble. Tell you what. I'll take Winston with me if that will make you feel better."

"Take your pistol as well. That will make me feel even better."

"Okay, but I think you're overreacting."

"I'd like to think so, but I remember a few other times when having a pistol and Winston would have been a lot better for you, but you didn't think you needed them. Humor me, please?"

"Just for you. What's on your schedule tomorrow?"

"Lewis Jefferson called and asked me to meet him at his office. Evidently the employee of his who wasn't at work today called him tonight and told Lewis he'd seen some people out in the forest yesterday in the area where they were conducting logging operations. He said it was late in the afternoon. He didn't think anything about it until he saw on the news tonight that someone had been murdered on the company's property. He didn't want to tell Lewis exactly what he'd seen over the phone, so Lewis thought since he was meeting him at the office tomorrow, I probably should be there too."

"Roger, please call me after the meeting if you think it's anything I should be aware of. You know I'm trying to help Seth, and I'm trying to help Gertie as well."

"I certainly didn't know when we were introduced at my law office in San Francisco that I'd end up marrying an amateur sleuth who had a talent for almost getting herself killed while investigating a murder. I sure didn't see that one coming."

"Sounds like you're having second thoughts about having married me."

"Not in the least, Liz. I just love you too much to have anything happen to you, so being manly and all, I'm trying to do whatever I can to protect my woman."

"Roger, I love it when you go caveman," she said as she warmly kissed him. Winston knew when he wasn't wanted and walked down the hall to Roger's office and his dog bed.

CHAPTER FIFTEEN

As soon as Roger left for the office the following morning, Liz sat down at the computer in her office. She wanted to see if Ruby Myers was on Facebook and if so, what she looked like. She was afraid that if she was avoiding her husband and the chief of police, there was a good chance she'd try to avoid Liz as well. She pulled up Ruby's Facebook page and saw a photo of an attractive red-haired woman. She spent a few moments reading about her and looking at her page. There was nothing unusual on it, certainly nothing that hinted of being tied to a murder. Liz read that she was married to George Myers and worked for the California Forestry Service. She had several inspirational sayings on her page and photographs of her mother as well as some colleagues at work. She posted rather sporadically, and the last one was two weeks old.

Hmm, that red hair would be hard to hide. I'm glad I had a chance to see her photograph. At least if she opens the door and pretends Ruby isn't home, I'll know she is. And the name Ruby. With all that red hair, I bet that's why her parents named her Ruby. Better see if I can find anything out about her mother, Joyce Samuels.

She cleared her computer screen and then pulled up Joyce Samuels on Facebook. She saw a photo of a rather nondescript looking woman with mousy brown hair, about fifty years old, and from the photograph, it looked to Liz like she carried too much weight.

Ruby must have gotten her hair from her father. Says here that her mother is divorced and works as a checker at the Pleasantville Market. She posts even less than her daughter.

Liz got dressed and called out to Winston. "Come on, boy, we're off to Pleasantville." He wagged his tail as if he knew exactly what she was saying as he jumped in the van.

Twenty minutes later she saw the sign for Pleasantville. Seth had been right. The town consisted of a main street with several stores, a small cafe, and a gas station. Liz guessed the population couldn't have been more than 1,000 people. There were only a few streets intersecting the main street, and she easily found Center Street and the address Seth had given her.

She parked her van about a block from the address and walked to the house which was just as nondescript as the owner. It was clearly in need of some tender loving care. Grey paint was peeling off the siding, and the window screens were torn. Weeds had taken over the lawn, and the walkway and steps leading up to the house were badly cracked.

Liz knew Roger wouldn't approve of her leaving Winston in the van, but she didn't think a menacing looking big boxer was going to help get Ruby or her mother to open the door for her. Although the street was very quiet she heard the soft sounds of a television coming from inside the house. She knew someone was probably home, she just didn't know who. Liz knocked on the door, and a few moments later it was partially opened by a woman who resembled the photograph of Joyce Samuels she had seen on Facebook.

"Mrs. Samuels, my name is Liz Langley. I'd like to speak with your daughter, Ruby Myers. I know the manager of the local Forest Service office, and he's concerned because he hasn't heard from Ruby today, and she didn't show up for work."

"Don't know nothin' about that. Haven't seen Ruby for a couple of weeks. Have you tried her husband? She's probably at home, playing hooky. Poor girl works so hard she needs a day off from time to time. No, can't help you," she said shutting the door.

Liz had no choice but to walk back to her van. She got in and petted Winston. "Well, Winston, I want to go to that gallery I saw yesterday, but I have a feeling if I wait here a little while, Ruby may show up. Evidently she's not going home to George, and from her Facebook page it doesn't seem like she has a lot of close friends or family members. Looks like her mama may be it for her, and George told Seth he saw her car here. Think we'll just sit here for awhile and see what happens. Lie down, big guy, and make yourself comfortable."

CHAPTER SIXTEEN

Liz sipped the coffee she'd brought with her and opened the gourmet food magazine she'd thrown in the van just as they were leaving. Forty-five minutes later she heard the sound of a car approaching. She looked up from her magazine and saw a nondescript grey car turn into Mrs. Samuel's driveway. The engine stopped, and moments later an attractive red-haired young woman got out of the car and quickly entered the house. *Bingo*, Liz thought, opening the van door and walking up the sidewalk.

When she got to the porch she knocked on the door. There were no sounds coming from within the house. Even the television had been muted. Liz knocked again and said in a loud voice, "Ruby, I know you're in there. I saw you go in the house. I want to talk to you. I'm not with any law enforcement organization, but if you don't open the door, I'll have to call the chief of police over in Red Cedar and if I do that, he'll be here shortly. Please open the door."

She waited and decided to count to ten before she left to call Seth. When she got to seven Ruby opened the door. "Who are you, and what do you want?" she asked.

"My name is Liz Langley, and I'm a good friend of the owner of Gertie's Diner over in Red Cedar. Her step-brother, David Sanders, was murdered yesterday. I'm trying to help her find the killer."

"Ruby, I know you're the one who called the chief of police about David Sanders' death. I want to help you. Please tell me what you know. Every hour that goes by makes it much harder for his killer to be caught."

The attractive redhead wiped tears from her eyes and said in a quiet voice, "Come in. I'll tell you what I know, but you have to promise me you won't tell my husband I'm here."

"I promise you I won't, but I think he already knows," Liz said as she entered the living room. Ruby motioned for her to sit down in a chair and she took a seat across from her.

"What do you want from me?" Ruby asked.

"I want to know how you found David and what you can tell me about that."

Ruby wrung her hands together and began to speak in a shaky voice, "I never should have left the office yesterday to meet David. There was always something about him I couldn't resist and sure enough, when he asked me to meet him at the lumber company's property where he was going to look for a blue butterfly, I said yes. I knew it was a bad decision as soon as I'd said it, but it was as if it was out of my hands. He always did have that kind of effect on me."

"I understand you left the forestry office about a half an hour after he did. Does that sound about right?"

"Yes. I didn't want people to think I was meeting him. My husband is a very jealous man, and I knew if he even suspected I was meeting David, George would kill him."

"Let me ask you something. Do you really think your husband is capable of killing someone?"

"Yes. When we met he had a terrible temper and often acted on it. I refused to marry him until he got some psychological help which he did. He hasn't had a temper incident for months, but that doesn't mean I don't think he could."

"All right. Tell me how you found David. When you got to the lumber company's property, what happened? Did you talk to David?"

"No. I parked my car and walked up the trail. I heard the sounds of chainsaws and trees being cut, and I knew there must be some people nearby. I was concerned someone would see me and tell my husband. I waited for a few minutes until the sounds began to lessen. When they did, I figured they were cutting in another direction. I walked to the place where I was supposed to meet David, and when I got there his body was on the ground surrounded by a pool of blood. I didn't know what to do. I was panicked, so I ran back to my car and drove away as fast as I could."

"Did you see any cars in the parking lot that you recognized?" Liz asked.

Ruby looked down at her hands and then away from Liz.

"I don't think you had anything to do with David's death, Ruby, but if I'm going to help you, I need to know everything. What aren't you telling me?"

Ruby stood up and began to pace the length of the room. Finally she spoke in a soft voice, "I recognized George's car. There was no one in it. I'm sure it was his car, because he has a San Francisco Giants bumper sticker on his car. He's a huge fan, and I always told him that everyone would know it was his car because of the sticker, so he better not get in any trouble. We used to laugh about it, but he refused to get rid of it. It was definitely George's car." She started sobbing.

"You're afraid of him, aren't you?" Liz asked.

"Of course I am. In fact I'm more than afraid, actually, I'm terrified. He had to have seen my car in the parking lot, and David was driving a Forest Service car, so he could easily put two and two together and assume I was meeting David."

"Ruby, he knows you're here. He called the chief of police and told him he'd seen your car here at your mother's house. If you're afraid of him, and based on what you're telling me, I think you probably need to go somewhere until the murder is solved, and he's either cleared or arrested. Right now the only thing he has against him is you testifying that you saw his car in a parking lot. I'm married to a man who has been a criminal defense attorney for thirty years, and from what he's told me, I doubt that would be enough evidence for him to be arrested for David's murder."

"I don't know where I can go."

"Wait a minute. I have an idea. You lived with David in his apartment in Sacramento before you came to Red Cedar. Isn't that right?"

"Yes. We were there for almost two years. Why?"

"Well, I may be sticking my neck out here, but I don't think you were involved in David's murder. I talked to Mitch Stevenson yesterday, and he was going to have David's apartment cleared out and cleaned by a cleaning woman who works for him. Why don't I call him and tell him that you're going to spend a few days there until this situation is taken care of?"

"That would be wonderful. I'm really afraid of George. I think there's a good chance he killed David, and I think there's a good chance he'll try to kill me, but you don't even know me. Why are you doing all of this for me?"

"Gertie told me she really likes you. She's my friend and as you know, David's step-sister. I think if the killer isn't found pretty fast, the chief of police will charge Gertie with the murder. I feel certain she didn't do it, and I want to help her. Is there anything else you can tell me about when you discovered David?"

"No. I didn't even get close to him. I was terrified, and the first thing that came to mind was to get out of there, even more so when I saw George's car. I called my mother from my car, and she said I could come to her place and stay with her. I couldn't sleep all night, and that's when I called the chief of police. I didn't want David's body to be eaten by animals. I should have called the chief night before last, but I was so distraught I wasn't thinking very straight. My mother had her hands full trying to keep me calm."

"Ruby, if you're so afraid of George, why did you leave the house this morning?"

"My bank has a branch in the next town over from here. I went there and cashed a check. I wasn't sure how long I could stay with my mother before George came, and I thought I'd probably need some money."

"That makes sense. When I leave here I'll call Mitch about you staying in David's apartment. He seems trustworthy, and I'll tell him why. I'll ask him to get the key from the apartment manager and leave it under the door mat for you. Here's my telephone number. If you think of anything, please let me know. I'd also like your number."

"Of course." Ruby quickly jotted down her cell phone number on the back of a business card and handed it to Liz. "I'm going to leave as soon as I say goodbye to my mother. I'll call you later today when I get to the apartment. Again, thanks for everything. Please tell Gertie how sorry I am about this."

"I will. Be safe." Liz turned and walked out the door. When she got to her van she called Mitch and explained what had happened. He assured her no one would know about Ruby, and he would personally make sure the apartment key would be under the door mat. When Liz's thoughts turned to Gertie and Ruby, and there wasn't any sign of the niggle, she started to drive back towards Red Cedar.

CHAPTER SEVENTEEN

Liz was glad she'd been able to help Ruby. The niggle was nowhere to be found when she thought about Ruby, and that was an encouraging sign. She was certain the only crime Ruby had been guilty of was agreeing to see a past lover while she was married, and of course that wasn't a crime at all. Unfortunately the man she was married to had a violent temper according to several people. She dreaded talking to Ruby's husband, George Myers, but she knew if she was going to solve David Sanders' murder, it had to be done. She looked at the address Seth had given her, googled it on her cell phone, and began driving to his residence.

The one story house was medium-sized for the area with blooming flowers lining the walkway that led to the porch where someone had planted several oak tubs that spilled over with brightly colored plants and flowers. Several different kinds of ferns hung from the porch overhang. Although she hadn't met George Myers, the bright colors seemed to be something that would fit more with his redheaded wife than him.

Liz decided to take Winston with her. She wasn't sure how she would be received by George Myers and hoped that the sight of the big dog would cause him to think twice about doing anything other than talking to her. She rang the doorbell.

A few moments later the door was opened by a large unkempt

man who looked like he hadn't slept recently. His eyes were bloodshot, and the t-shirt he wore was stained. His hair was standing on end and in urgent need of some extensive grooming. His nose looked like it had been broken and badly set. From what she'd heard about his past, that didn't surprise her. Although Liz didn't feel particularly threatened by him, he was not a pleasant sight. "What do you want?" the man asked in a harsh challenging tone of voice.

"I'm Liz Langley, and I assume you're George Myers. I work with the police chief, Seth Williams. He told me you'd called him several times regarding your wife who seems to be missing. I'd like to talk to you, so we can start the procedures for filing a missing person report. Seth had some other things that needed to be taken care of today, and he asked me to come in his place. May my dog and I come in?"

"I don't like dogs much. Why does he have to come in?"

"Unfortunately I have a medical condition, and he's a therapy dog. My doctor insists I keep him with me at all times."

"Well, in that case I guess he can come in. Is he housebroken?" George asked as he opened the door for Liz and Winston.

"Yes, and he won't leave my side. I'll only be a few minutes," she said sitting down in a chair he indicated with a wave of his hand while Winston sat next to her. "Please tell me everything you know about your wife's disappearance. You might want to start with the last time you saw her."

George put his head in his hands and was quiet for several long moments. Finally he looked up at Liz, sighed, and began to talk, "I came home for lunch day before yesterday, just as I usually do. We kind of had a loose arrangement of meeting at home for lunch. Ruby was here before me, and when I came in we talked for awhile. She left to go back to work at the Forestry Service office, and I left to go to my job at the lumber mill. That was the last time I saw her," he said visibly distraught.

As he spoke to Liz, his voice shook, and he nervously wrung his hands together. He continued, "She never came home that night. Yesterday I went over to Pleasantville where her mother lives, and I saw Ruby's car in the driveway. I went up to the door and rang the bell, but no one answered it. It was as if she was avoiding me for some reason. I went back to her mother's house yesterday afternoon, but Ruby's car wasn't there. I don't know what's happened to her."

"Mr. Myers, did you have an argument with her? Could there be some other reason she might be avoiding you?" Liz said thinking of David and his former relationship with Ruby. "Could her mother be protecting her for some reason?"

"If she is I don't know why," he said in a ragged voice. "Her mother's never liked me, and she barely agreed to come to our wedding. She didn't think I was good enough for her daughter, but I've been a very good husband to Ruby. I can't figure out why she's avoiding me."

I think I can, Liz thought, *but it probably would be premature for me to say anything.*

"Mr. Myers, since you didn't see Ruby when you went back to her mother's home yesterday, is there a chance she's left and gone somewhere else?"

"I don't know. All I want is for Ruby to come back home."

"Has she ever done anything like this in the past?"

"Never. We've been married for six months, and it's been the happiest and best time of my life. I thought it was for her too. Now I don't know what to make of her disappearance."

"I hate to ask this, Mr. Myers, but have you ever given her reason to fear you? It's been my experience that if a woman doesn't want her husband to find her, often it's because she's afraid of him."

"No. I've never threatened her, and I've never touched her in anger. I'm one of the mildest people in the world. I can't remember the last time I was angry about anything."

"Let me change the subject. You mentioned you work at the lumber mill. Why aren't you there today?"

"I can't face up to going to work until I find Ruby. I didn't go in yesterday. Look at me. I'm a mess without her. I've got to find her. Please help me."

"I'll see what I can do. I believe you mentioned to the police chief that Ruby sometimes went to a bar after work. What's the name of it? Maybe someone there knows something."

"It's the Last Chance Saloon. I called there night before last to see if she'd been there that night, but they said they hadn't seen her. I dunno. Maybe they were protecting her or something."

Liz stood up and put out her hand. "I'll see what I can do about finding Ruby. If you think of any reason why she may be avoiding you, please call me. It might help me find her."

"Yeah, you'll be the first to know after I talk to her."

Liz looked him squarely in the eye. For a brief moment she saw rage in his eyes, and then they reverted to the puppy like quality she'd seen in them when she first entered the house. "Mr. Myers, if she doesn't want to see you at the moment, I'd advise you to give up your search until this problem is solved. If she's afraid of you for some reason and finds out you're searching for her, it might cause her to continue to stay away or do something stupid which could result in her being hurt."

He muttered something under his breath, and Liz swore he said, "The only person that might hurt her is me when I find her."

"Mr. Myers, let me caution you again to let the professionals do what they're trained to do. The police chief has made her disappearance a priority, and I'm sure we'll find her. Thanks for taking the time to talk to me. Winston, come," she said, and the two of them walked out the front door and over to her van.

After she and Winston had gotten in the van she turned to Winston and said, "Either George Myers has his head in the sand, or he's hiding something, and it's up to me to find out which one it is."

CHAPTER EIGHTEEN

"Winston, we've got a little time before I have to get back to the lodge and get ready for dinner tonight. I remember seeing that art gallery across from the parking lot out by the Jefferson timber property. I think we need to go there and see if I can find something for the lodge."

Winston thumped his tail in complete agreement. Red Cedar was a small town, and George lived only a few minutes from the Markham Gallery, so the drive to the gallery was short. Liz glanced at her watch and saw it was almost noon. *Good*, she thought, *I'm sure the gallery will be open by now*. After she parked in the lot she noticed there was an OPEN sign on the front door of the gallery. When she opened the door a bell tinkled, and an attractive woman entered the room through a piece of cloth that had been hung up to separate the front of the building from the back.

"Hi. I'm Joan Markham. Welcome to my gallery. Sorry for my appearance, but I'm working on a painting," she said laughing as she pointed to the paint-spattered smock she was wearing. Liz immediately liked the dark-haired woman with the greyest eyes Liz had ever seen. Her hair was pulled away from her face and swept up in a ponytail. Even though she appeared to be in her early 40's, an age when most women wouldn't consider wearing their hair in a ponytail, on Joan Markham it seemed perfectly natural.

"Well, if you're busy painting, I assume that most of the paintings I see on the walls are by you. Would that be correct?"

"Yes. I suppose some people would say it's an exercise in vanity, but I always wanted a gallery where I could display my art, and a few years ago I asked myself what I was waiting for. My parents owned this property, and it became mine when they died. The building we're in was originally their home. I converted the front into an art gallery, and I live in the back."

"You probably know Gertie of Gertie's Diner. I was driving by here the other day with her, and she mentioned that you display your work at a gallery in San Francisco as well as here," Liz said as she walked around the room admiring the paintings that were on display. "You're very good. I like how you've brought people into the landscapes and seascapes of Northern California. The effect is quite stunning. How did you come up with that particular way of doing art?"

"People fascinate me. Some of my first memories include me trying to capture what a person looked like by drawing them on paper. It continued as I got older. I rarely forget a face, and I like to paint people as they appear in natural settings. With so much beauty around here, I try to preserve it through my paintings. I don't know if it will be here forever. I suppose it's my way of giving back to the universe.

"To change the subject, yes, I do know Gertie, and I heard about her step-brother's death. Please tell her how sorry I am. I don't know her well, but occasionally I go to her diner for a hamburger and chocolate malt. I know I shouldn't," she said patting her stomach, "but it's as if my stomach has a mind of its own on those occasions, and my only job is to listen to it. I heard her step-brother was murdered somewhere on the timber property just across the road."

"Yes. Actually, I'm helping the police chief try to solve the murder. For some reason I've found myself embroiled in some other murders, and I've been able to solve them, so Chief Williams asked if I'd help him with this one."

"When was he murdered?" Joan asked.

"Probably late in the afternoon the day before yesterday. Why?"

"Maybe I can help you," she said. Joan walked over to a desk on the far side of the gallery and opened a drawer. "I have this compelling urge to take photographs of everyone who visits the parking lot across the road, whether they're hikers, lumberjacks, or whatever. When I find a face that appeals to me, I incorporate it into one of my paintings. I use the photographs as a starting point for my art, although I do change the features a bit so the person isn't easily recognizable. I don't want to be sued for invasion of privacy. I suppose someone who knows the person might say that the painting bears a resemblance to so-and-so, but I think that's as far as it would ever go.

"The photographs are dated and have the time of day on them, so I know exactly when they were taken. I remember taking some that afternoon. Let me see what I have," she said, pulling a stack of photographs out of the desk drawer and leafing through them.

"That could be a huge help to me," Liz said. "It doesn't necessarily mean that just because someone's photograph was taken here on that particular afternoon that they had anything to do with the murder, but they might have seen something. I really appreciate it. Thanks."

"Here. I found five photographs. There's a young woman who left by herself, and about twenty minutes later a young man left. This photograph is of a man who struck me as being unhealthy. You can see from his photograph he looks very pale, and he's a little too young to be that stoop-shouldered. Here's one which is probably Gertie's step-brother, because he's wearing a Forest Service uniform, and the last one here is a photograph of a man who looked angry to me. I hope they're of some help to you."

"Thank you so much. I'm not sure how I'll find these people, but Red Cedar isn't all that big, so someone should know them unless they're from out of town." Liz glanced down at the photographs and involuntarily gasped.

"What's wrong?" Joan asked.

"Well, this is almost uncanny. I recognize this man. In fact I just came from his home, and he didn't say anything about being here. This photo confirms what his wife told me when she said she'd seen his car in the parking lot across the road."

"I wouldn't know anything about that. You're welcome to keep the photographs. None of the people has the type of face I'm looking for to include in my artwork. As I said, taking these photographs is kind of a compulsive habit of mine."

"Thank you. I'd like to buy that piece hanging over in the corner," Liz said pointing to a painting of a woman hiking on a trail. "I own the Red Cedar Spa and Lodge, and guests often ask me what else there is to do around here. I could show them that painting and tell them about the trailheads located across the road on the U.S. Forest Service land. Even if I didn't own the spa, I'd probably buy this piece because it really speaks to me."

"Would you be open to a trade?" Joan asked. "I've been promising myself forever that I would visit your spa. I really need to take time off for some massages, because I tense up with concentration when I'm working on a painting, and lately my back has really been bothering me. I'd like to apply the money I'd get for the painting to spa treatments. Would that work for you?"

"Absolutely. When you call to make an appointment, ask to speak with Bertha. She's my manager, and I'll tell her about our arrangement."

"Great! Let me wrap the piece for you. I understand the dinners at the lodge are wonderful. I might have to work one of those in as well, and of course I've heard about the exploits of your dog, Brandy Boy, and how he carries brandy to cottage guests when one of them rings a bell," Joan said laughing.

"Let me know when you're coming, and I'll show you how to ring the bell so you can watch him in action," Liz said as she took the package from Joan. "Again, thank you. I really enjoyed meeting you and look forward to seeing you again." Liz walked out the door to the van where Winston was standing in the front seat, keeping the van safe from all intruders.

I know it's instinctual on his part, but you'd have to be crazy to try and break into my van with a guard dog like him standing there. She silently thanked Roger once again for giving Winston to her as a gift.

CHAPTER NINETEEN

When Liz opened the front door to the lodge, she realized she'd spent more time at the art gallery than she'd intended, and it was already mid-afternoon and time to get ready for tonight's dinner. Gina was sitting at the kitchen counter waiting for her.

"Sorry I'm late, Gina. I got tied up. I took some steaks out of the freezer before I left this morning, and I'm planning on having Roger cook them. Sunny days like today are pretty rare here on the coast so I might as well take advantage of it and use the barbecue. I'd like you to make my special recipe for twice baked potatoes and also some rosemary bread. Oh, and I'd like to serve a wedge salad with dinner. You can put the lettuce wedges on the plates along with a salad fork and chill them in the frig. Fry some bacon and crumble it. We've got bleu cheese and some ranch dressing I can put on right before we serve the salads. I'll take care of dessert, and I'll also prep some fresh asparagus. Go ahead and assemble a cheese platter and get some crackers out of the pantry. I think that should do it for now. Let's get started."

They worked silently for the next couple of hours. When they were nearly finished Liz said, "I'm going downstairs and get dressed. When I come back I'll open the wine and put the cheese and crackers out. How are you doing?"

"Fine. I finished everything you asked me to do. The only thing that's left is to clean up the kitchen before the guests arrive. Do you want me to start the barbecue?" Gina asked.

"No, when Roger left this morning I asked him if he'd mind barbecuing the steaks tonight, and he said he'd make sure that he was home in plenty of time to take care of it. Matter of fact, I think that's him now," Liz said as they heard a car pull into the lodge parking lot.

Liz opened the door and waved to him when he got out of his car. She kissed him on the cheek as he came through the door. "Perfect timing. You've got about half an hour until the guests arrive, and we'll eat about forty-five minutes after that. Don't forget you promised to barbecue steaks tonight, so you're in charge of getting the fire started. And last, but not least, how was your day?"

"Long. I need to change clothes and wash up. I'll be back in a few minutes."

"Take your time. I need to go down and get dressed, too. Everything's prepped and ready for dinner. I even have the mushroom caps ready to be sautéed in butter and garlic." Together they walked down the stairs.

"Liz, I don't have time to go into it now, but I made an appointment for you tomorrow with one of Lewis' lumberjacks. I met with him and Lewis today, but you need to talk to him. I think he might be of some help in the murder investigation. Hope you don't mind, but you're scheduled to meet him at 11:00 in my office. I'll tell you more after dinner."

"That definitely whets my curiosity. I have a few things to share with you as well. After dinner it is."

A few hours later after the last guest had left, Liz turned to Gina and said, "You've put in a long day, young lady. Thanks for everything. I had a lot of compliments on the twice baked potatoes and the salad. I think you're probably about ready to do a whole meal by yourself."

"Thanks for the vote of confidence, Liz, but I don't think I'm anywhere near ready for prime time. Don't even consider it. I'd be scared to death. Let me keep learning from you for a few more months before you trust me with anything like that. I'd hate for you to have a mass exodus from the cottages because of me preparing a really bad dinner or even worse, everyone getting sick from something I did or didn't do," Gina said laughing as she walked out the door. "See you tomorrow afternoon."

"Roger, why don't you go downstairs and unwind while you watch the nightly news. I'll take care of Brandy Boy and Winston. Since the cottages are full, I better make sure Brandy Boy has enough brandy in his cask to make his deliveries. I'm sure some of the guests will want to see our famous St. Bernard in action tonight. I'll be down in a few minutes."

*****

"Well, now that you've had time to take a few deep breaths and unwind a little, tell me what Lewis' employee had to say at your meeting today."

"I don't know what to make of any of it, but he said he saw several people near the scene of the murder on that afternoon. He recognized one of them because he's a Jefferson Lumber employee. Evidently he's the one I mentioned to you that has cancer. Apparently he's certain he got it from exposure to the formaldehyde that's used by Jefferson Lumber in the manufacture of their plywood. Think I told you Lewis is a little concerned that his manager got sloppy, and that the necessary safety precautions weren't taken care of properly. This employee's name is Mark Bailey. He also saw a younger man and a woman walking together near where David was murdered. A little later he said he saw a bearded man in a California Forestry uniform and lastly, a large man who, in Mark's words, looked like he was angry."

"Well, since he told you all that, why do you want me to see him? Do you think he's leaving something out?"

"No, but I think you might be able to get fuller descriptions of the people than he gave me. He didn't recognize any of the people other than the Jefferson employee, who appeared to be rather sickly. I've been thinking about him and as sick as he seems to be, it seems odd to me he'd go out to the Jefferson Lumber property. If he's going to sue Jefferson Lumber, I wouldn't think he'd want to be on their property. If he was my client, and I was going to file suit on his behalf, I'd tell him not to have anything to do with the company and to stay away from their property. I rather doubt his doctor would want him to physically exert himself by walking around out in the woods. I think he'd need all of his energy to be channeled into healing."

"I agree. I look forward to talking to Mark. Wait a minute. I just thought of something." She walked over to the desk and picked up her purse. "Roger, I told you I had an interesting day as well. I spent quite a bit of time with Ruby Myers. I'm sure you remember Gertie talking about Ruby's husband, George. She's the one that Seth told me was missing the night before David's body was discovered. After I met with Ruby I went to her husband's home and talked to him."

For the next half hour she described her meetings with both of them and how she'd made arrangements for Ruby to go to Sacramento and stay in David's apartment until there was some resolution of the situation.

"Wait a minute, Liz, are you telling me you went to George Myers' home after Ruby told you she was terrified of him? To say nothing of the fact that I seem to remember Gertie telling Seth that she knew he was the one who'd killed David?"

Liz squirmed a little in the chair she was sitting in and tried to avoid Roger's eyes, and then started speaking very rapidly. "Roger, I knew you wouldn't be happy about me going to see George, so I took Winston with me. I don't think George is a dog person, because he was very cool to Winston and really didn't want him to come into his house. I told him Winston was a therapy dog, and my doctor insisted he be with me at all times. I also had my gun in my purse."

"Swell, that's just swell. Oh, Liz, what am I going to do with you? Not only did you go to the home of someone who is known to have had a bad temper in the past, but you also just alerted him to the fact that you're probably working with the police chief to help him solve the murder. It's pretty easy to go on the Internet and see where you've been involved in solving them before. If he's the killer, now he's aware you might know something, and he may feel he needs to kill you. Liz, this may call for more than Winston and a gun."

"Well, Roger, as a matter of fact I do know something. I know that George Myers is a liar, and that he was out near the scene of the murder about the time David was killed."

He raised an eyebrow and said, "Since he didn't tell you that, how could you know?"

Liz told him about her meeting with Joan Markham and the photographs she'd given to Liz. She took them out of her purse and handed them to Roger. "See the man in this one? That's George Myers. Joan took his photograph as he was walking to his car. There are three other photographs of people who could be considered suspects. Joan commented that this man didn't look very healthy," Liz said as she pointed to one of the photographs. "Maybe he's the one from Jefferson Lumber. If he is, then maybe the man I'm going to meet in your office tomorrow can identify him. If he can, and if it's him, that would leave two of the people in the photographs still unidentified, namely the young woman and the young man. I don't know how I can find out who they are."

"For whatever it's worth, Liz, I have the utmost confidence in you, and I'm sure you'll find a way to do it. What I do ask is that you don't go anywhere without Winston and your gun. From now on I'd like you to keep the front door of the lodge locked. I know you usually keep it open in case a guest wants to come in and use their laptop or tablet to access the Internet since there isn't any Wi-Fi in the cottages, but that needs to be changed. Matter of fact, why don't you leave a note on the door that you're changing the open door policy, and from now on guests will have to ring the doorbell or knock. I don't think anyone would find that unusual, and it just might save your life."

"You're not making me feel very good. I prefer to look at the world as a glass half-full. I'm getting the distinct feeling you're looking at it as a glass half-empty."

"I prefer to think of it as being realistic, a word I don't think you're particularly familiar with, and one you might want to make use of a bit more," he said scowling.

"Okay, I get the message. I promise I'll be very careful. I think as long as I'm going into your office tomorrow I'll stop by the diner and talk to Gertie. She knows everything that's happening in this town. Maybe something's happened I don't know about. Looks like a busy day. Ready for bed?"

"Lady, I thought you'd never ask! That's the first thing you've said in an hour that appeals to me. Lead the way."

CHAPTER TWENTY

A few minutes before 11:00 the next morning Liz parked her van in front of Roger's office, let Winston out, and the two of them walked into his law office. She nodded to a man sitting in the reception area who was wearing a plaid flannel shirt, jeans, and heavy boots. "Morning, Jessica. Would you tell Roger I'm here?" she said to Roger's secretary. Jessica had been with Roger for a number of years, and when he'd decided to open the office in Red Cedar as a branch office of his San Francisco law firm, Jessica had told him that since she wasn't married and didn't have children, if it was all right with him, she'd like to continue working for him and move to Red Cedar.

Roger was really happy she'd made that decision. He'd even told Liz he hesitated to open a law office in Red Cedar, because he'd have to train a new secretary, and he'd said he was spoiled by having had an excellent one like Jessica for so many years. Fortunately it had worked out to everyone's advantage.

Jessica buzzed Roger and told him that Liz and Mark Bailey were both in the office. A moment later Roger opened the door of his office. "Please come in," he said. "Liz, I'd like you to meet Mark Bailey with Jefferson Lumber Company. Mark, this is my wife Liz, and our dog, Winston. He's a guard dog I got for Liz, because I get a little paranoid about some of the things Liz finds herself involved in. I'm the one who insists she take Winston with her everywhere she goes. Please sit down. Would you like some coffee or water?"

Liz and Mark declined, and Roger began to speak, "Mark, when we talked yesterday you mentioned on the day David Sanders was murdered, you were in the area where he was killed. As I understand it, you were getting ready to log some trees on the Jefferson Lumber Company property. You told me you saw several people that were also in the area on that day. Through a quirk of fate, Liz was able to obtain photographs of some people who were in that area about the same time as the murder. There are four photographs and each one is dated and time stamped as well. I'd like you to take a look at them, and see if you can identify any of the people in the photographs."

Liz handed him the photos and sat back to observe his reaction. He turned over three of them, but when he looked at the fourth photo he said, "The man in this photograph is Brad Cassidy. He works for Jefferson Lumber Company. Brad has cancer and is quite ill. He's been unable to work for several months."

"I'm not surprised he has cancer," Roger said. "When I saw the photograph I thought the man in it looked very unhealthy. What else can you tell me about him?"

Mark was quiet for a few moments and then looked at Roger and said, "Since you're a lawyer, if I say something you can't tell Lewis Jefferson about it, right? Isn't there something about an attorney-client privilege?"

"No, the attorney-client privilege doesn't apply here, because you're not my client. However, you have my word that whatever is said in this office will go no farther. I promise you I won't repeat it to Lewis."

Mark looked first at Roger and then at Liz. "A lot of us don't feel good about what's happened to Brad. In fact, the feeling is kind of like 'there but for the grace of God go I.' We're thinking any of us could have been working in the plywood plant where Brad worked and could have gotten cancer from the formaldehyde. People know the manager was pretty sloppy about a lot of things. Brad's family is having a tough time making ends meet without him being able to work and bring home a pay check, so a bunch of us have been passing the hat around every week after we get our paychecks to help him and his family. Becky, his wife, is working two jobs, and they have two little boys. It's really a bad situation. He's very bitter and angry about the whole thing."

"That's so sad, Mark. I feel for the family, but I am curious, since he looks so ill, why he would have been out at the Jefferson property on the day David Sanders was murdered. I'd think he would need to do everything he could to conserve his strength," Liz said.

"I have no idea why he would have been there. He's not a logger, and the land he was on is being logged. When I thought I'd seen him the other day I was sure I'd made a mistake, but based on this photograph it looks like it was him."

"I suppose the only thing I can do is ask him why he was there. Maybe something is going on that we know nothing about. Do you know where he lives?" Liz asked.

"Yes," Mark said hesitantly as he looked at Roger. "Don't want Lewis to know this, but I'm the one that's been taking the money we collect to Brad's house. He's a proud man, so I've been leaving it in an envelope in their mailbox. I'm pretty sure he wouldn't take it from me. This way it's just anonymous money that shows up in his mailbox every week. Here's where he lives." He looked at the contacts list on his cell phone and wrote down Brad's address.

"Thanks. I won't say who gave me his address," Liz said. "Matter of fact I'll bet if I show the photo to Gertie at the diner next door she'll probably tell me it's a photo of Brad Cassidy. I can say I looked his address up in a phone book. No, I promise my visit won't be traced to you. Can you tell me anything about the people in the other photos?"

"Not a thing. I don't recognize any of them in these other photographs. Wish I could help you more."

"Actually, Mark, you've been a big help," Liz said. "I'll go out to Brad's home and talk to him after I stop by Gertie's. Maybe he saw something that would help us while he was out in the area where the crime occurred. Also, I'm very curious as to why he went there given the status of his poor health. Thanks for meeting me here."

"Brad's a good man. A lot of the guys are pretty upset about the way his cancer treatment is being handled by Jefferson Lumber Company. If jobs were easier to come by, I think a lot of the guys would look elsewhere, but everybody's afraid of being out of work and with everything that's happened in the lumber industry in the last few years, we're all lucky to have a job."

CHAPTER TWENTY-ONE

Liz and Winston left Roger's office after their meeting with Mark Bailey and walked next door to Gertie's Diner. Liz would have asked Roger to join them, but she remembered him saying he was having lunch at the country club with a new client and as Roger told her, a man who could be a very important client.

"Well, well, well, ain't you two a sight for sore eyes," the irascible owner of the diner said. "Don't want the county breathin' down my neck 'bout allowin' a dog in here so, I bought a little somethin' fer Winston. Says therapy dog on it. Saw it at a garage sale the other day and thought of Winston. Usually we gots to hide him under the table, but now he can sit right out in public, proud as punch." She knelt down and put a harness holding a small sign that said "Therapy Dog" around Winston's massive chest. Gertie stood up and said, "Now he's legal as can be. Come on over to this here table. You'll have a good view of everybody that way. Got any news 'bout David?"

"Thanks for the harness, Gertie, he looks perfectly natural in it. As gentle as he is I wouldn't be surprised if he'd been some type of a therapy dog in another life. As to David, if you have a minute, I'd like to talk to you."

"When it comes to you, honey, I'll make time. What about his apartment? Gettin' that cleaned?"

86

"Well, I've had to hold up on that for a few days. It's nothing you need to worry about, but since David was killed and you're his step-sister, I think it's better for you if there are some things I don't tell you. They may be important in his case, and I don't want anyone thinking you know something and then maybe they'd go after you. We still don't really know what the motive was."

"Honey," Gertie said laughing, "If you think I can't pertect myself, you gots another think comin'. Been doin' it long before you were a gleam in your daddy's eye, and I plan on doin' it for a long time to come, but I appreciate the thought."

"Is there something more you can tell me about David? I know he worked for the California Forestry Service. He was jealous that your mother's Will left you what he thought was his father's money, and that he was single. I also know he had a relationship with Ruby Myers, but that's about it."

Gertie looked down at her hands and was uncharacteristically quiet, and then she slowly began to speak. "Never really knew him that well. Tol' ya' I'm twenty years older than he was. I got married when I was seventeen and never did live with my mother again, and I never did live in the same household with him. Sure, I'd see him from time to time when I went to visit her, but after she died we didn't have much to say to one another. We was kind of like oil and water, plus David never could play very well with the other kids in the sandbox, if ya' know what I mean. He was what I think's called a control freak. Probably why no woman stuck around for long. Man had drop dead killer good looks, I'll grant you that. Matter of fact, from what I heard, don't think he ever met a temptation he could resist."

"Sounds like even though you didn't know him very well you didn't think very much of him."

"Yeah, that's what I've been tellin' ya. He coulda been killed fer a number of reasons, none of which I know."

"Thanks. I think I have a better understanding of your

relationship with him, and I'm sure not hearing anything that would lead someone to suspect you." Liz took the photographs Joan Markham had given to her out of her purse, handed them to Gertie and said, "Gertie, I'd like you to look at these photographs that were taken near the murder scene at about the time David was murdered and tell me if you know any of these people."

A moment later Gertie looked up. "This here one is Ruby's husband, George. Tol' that fat police chief to start with him if he wanted to find the killer. I jes' know he done it. And now yer' tellin' me he was near the scene of the murder at 'bout the time it happened? Why're ya' lookin' any further? I'm bettin' my last hamburger and malt on him."

"I agree that's some powerful circumstantial evidence, but it doesn't necessarily make him the killer. That's not the kind of evidence that will stand up in a court of law."

"Well, maybe we need to have us some ol' fashioned country justice and jes' lynch the no-good son-of-a-gun. Ya' know, some of the guys that hang out here at the diner could form a little posse and bye-bye Georgie." She put her hands around her neck and made a choking noise. "Got me a few friends who'd be more than happy to do a favor fer Gertie. Lord knows, done a lot of favors for 'em. Maybe it's time fer me to call in some chits that are owed to me."

"No, I definitely don't think that's a good idea. Remember, one of the reasons I'm looking into this for you is because Chief Williams thinks of you as a suspect. I sure don't want to give him any additional ammunition. I've got some other things going on, Gertie, so just sit on this for awhile."

"Easy fer' ya' to say, honey, ain't yer' hiney that's lookin' at goin' to the slammer. May have wanted to do the nasty to David a few times over the years, but I got me some good morals, and killin' my step-brother jes' don't fit inta my lifestyle."

"I believe you, Gertie, I really do. To change the subject, as long as I'm here I probably better have a hamburger and a chocolate malt.

It would be a shame to let this opportunity pass me by."

"Now yer' talkin' some sense, honey. Gonna give big boy here a little hamburger that one of the customers couldn't finish. Ya' don't have a problem with that do ya'?"

"No, and I rather doubt Winston will either. Thanks, Gertie. Want me to take the harness with me or leave it at the reception desk?"

"Leave it. From now on, he'll be legit whenever he comes in. Don't know how yer' husband will take it, him bein' a lawyer sworn to uphold the law and all."

"Gertie, I don't think that's a problem. I imagine Roger will look the other way when Winston is wearing his therapy dog harness. Thanks again, and I'll be in touch. Just don't do anything without contacting me first."

"Won't, honey. Was jes' jawin' to make me feel better. Ain't the best of times fer me."

"I'm sure it's not," Liz said, "but I have a little niggle, and it's telling me we're getting closer to finding out who murdered David. Like I've told you before, if you think of something, let me know."

CHAPTER TWENTY-TWO

"Okay, Winston, just because now you can be a legal regular at Gertie's, don't be getting any ideas about being welcome in other public places. A lot of people don't want to see dogs in a restaurant, plus I'm pretty sure there are laws about having dogs in eating establishments. You're lucky you've got Gertie for a friend. I need to make one more stop, and then we'll go home."

Liz drove to the far side of Red Cedar and into a residential area of small sad-looking homes. Little attention or money had been spent on their upkeep, and there was a depressing feeling to the neighborhood. She found the address that Mark had given her for Brad Cassidy and parked on the street in front of his house. The neighborhood had been built before sidewalks were mandatory and without the benefit of a curb, weed choked lawns spilled into the street.

"I promised Roger I'd take you everywhere I go, so let's use the therapy dog excuse again, but to make it look legitimate, I'm going to put you on a leash," she said as she got out of her van and opened the door for Winston. As soon as he was on the street she put his leash on him.

The walkway leading to the house was badly cracked and weeds threatened to completely overtake the little cement that could be seen. She looked up at the house and saw where sheets had been hung in the windows in place of curtains. The house was badly in need of paint, and a tarp that was draped over half of the roof indicated there had been a roof leak which the Cassidy family couldn't afford to repair.

She knocked on the door, and it was answered by Brad Cassidy. She recognized him from the photograph Joan Markham had given her. Her niggle was absolutely silent, and as ill as this man looked she found it hard to believe he could have had the strength to be involved in any way with David Sanders' death.

"Mr. Cassidy, my name is Liz Langley. I'm helping Police Chief Seth Williams with a criminal investigation. I'd like to talk to you for a few minutes if you're feeling up to it."

He looked her up and down and then said, "Why would you assume I wouldn't be up to talking to you?" he asked.

"If you'll let me in, I'll tell you all about it."

"All right. I'm curious about why you're here, but I'll have to ask you to leave the dog outside. My wife's allergic to dogs."

"That's not a problem." She turned to Winston and said, "Sit. Stay." The big dog sat down on the front porch stoop, and Liz walked into the house. She didn't want to embarrass Brad, but she was appalled at how little furniture was in the front room. An old television was turned on, but the fuzzy shadowy images indicated it needed some work by a television repairman. There was a threadbare brown couch with a worn blanket on it where Liz assumed Brad spent most of his time. Two grey chairs looked like they'd been rescued from someone's yard just before the trash truck took them.

He closed the door behind him and said, "Would you tell me what this is about and how you know me?"

Liz sat down and in a soft and caring voice began to speak, "Mr. Cassidy, you have a lot of friends, and they're worried about you. I know you have cancer, and I've heard that you believe you got it from being exposed to formaldehyde at Jefferson Lumber Company when you were working there, but that's not why I'm here."

"How did you know all that?" he asked.

"It's not important. I'm trying to help the police chief, Seth Williams, find out who murdered a man by the name of David Sanders."

"Don't know anything about that. Television hasn't been working very good lately, and we don't take a paper, so I'm not really up to date on any recent news events. Who was he?"

"He was with the Forestry Service and was on the Jefferson Lumber property trying to confirm a sighting of a Lotis Blue butterfly which is on the Endangered Species List."

"I'm sorry, Mrs. Langley, but none of what you're saying seems to have anything to do with me. I have no idea what you're talking about."

She held up her hand. "Please, let me continue. Mr. Sanders was murdered three days ago late in the afternoon on some Jefferson Lumber Company property located on the far side of town. An anonymous person happened to be taking photographs of people who were in the area at that time. Your photograph was one of those taken, and you were standing next to a Jefferson Lumber Company sign. Could you tell me why you were on that property at that time?" She handed him the photograph that clearly showed he'd been on the property.

He looked at it for a few moments and then said, "That's me, and yes, I was there that day."

"Pardon me, Mr. Cassidy, but I understand you have cancer, and you're going through chemotherapy treatments at the present time. Why would you waste your limited strength and energy to go out to that property?"

Brad put his head in his hands, and a dry sob escaped from his throat. After several minutes he took his hands away from his face and looked at Liz. "When I found out I had cancer I wrote a letter to Mr. Jefferson telling him my doctor was certain I'd gotten it from the formaldehyde used at the plywood plant where I worked. The doctor felt the plant manager had not taken the necessary safety precautions required when people work with it. In my letter to Mr. Jefferson I told him I didn't plan on suing Jefferson Lumber, because I know what hard times the lumber companies have been going through recently. I didn't want the company to go out of business because of some big lawsuit. I have a lot of friends who work there, and I didn't want to be responsible for them losing their jobs."

"That's a much more caring attitude than most people would have had," Liz said.

"Well, be that as it may, I couldn't do it to my friends, but in my letter I asked Mr. Jefferson if he would pay my medical bills when my insurance ran out. There was a cap on the amount the insurance company would pay for cancer treatment, and I knew I was about to exceed it. He never answered my letter.

"I was in Afghanistan for two tours of duty, and I didn't think life could get much worse than what I experienced when I was over there. I was so glad to come home, be with my family, and have a good job. But life took a turn for the worse when I got this cancer, and now I feel like my life is getting about as bad as it was over there."

Brad looked at Liz and continued, "Becky, she's my wife, is working two jobs, and we still can't make ends meet. We're going farther and farther into debt every month. I don't know what will happen to her and the boys if I live, and I don't know what will happen to them if I die. I feel like I'm in a no-win situation that I didn't have anything to do with."

"I'm so sorry, Mr. Cassidy," Liz said putting her hand on his arm, "but I still don't understand what this has to do with why you were on the Jefferson Lumber property that afternoon."

"I was hooked up to the chemo drip when the idea came to me that if I talked to Mr. Jefferson in person I might be able to make him understand how desperate I was becoming. I knew I'd never get past his secretary if I went to his office. I remembered some of the guys saying that late every afternoon he went to the part of the forest where the trees had been logged that day to see what progress had been made and find out if there were any problems. I knew where they were logging, and I figured he'd be there."

"Did you have a chance to talk to him?"

"No. I waited for about thirty minutes, and then I felt so weak I was afraid I wouldn't be able to make it back home if I stayed any longer. I'd borrowed my mother-in-law's car because mine had been repossessed, and I sure didn't want to get in an accident. I left and never did see him."

"Did you see any other people there?"

"I saw a young couple, a man and a woman. The only other thing I remember seeing was a Forestry Service car in the parking lot. I was hurting pretty bad by then and just wanted to get home."

"I understand. Thank you for talking to me. I wish I could help you."

"Mrs. Langley, how did you know that the man in the photograph was me?"

"I showed that photo to a person that happened to know you, and that person gave me your name. I looked your name up in the phone book and got your address. Trust me, the person who gave me your name is someone who cares deeply for you and wants to help you. His way of helping was to assure me you had nothing to do with the murder of David Sanders, and he felt the best way to have your name cleared was for me to talk to you. I think he was right about you having nothing to do with the murder."

"That's for sure. I don't think I'd even have the energy to kill Mr.

Jefferson if he was sitting across from me, and I'd be far more inclined to do something like that rather than murder some guy who worked for the Forestry Service. Wouldn't make any sense."

Liz stood up and put out her hand. "I agree. I don't know what I can do for you, but I certainly will try and think of something. I know someone who has the ear of Lewis Jefferson. Maybe I can get him to help. Stay where you are. I'll let myself out." She stood up and walked over to the door.

"If you can do anything, I'd appreciate it. I know that worrying like I am isn't going to help the cancer go away, but it's about the only thing I can do."

"Good-bye Mr. Cassidy. For whatever it's worth, I'll be sending healing thoughts your way."

"Thanks," he said lying down on the couch. She closed the door softly behind her and shook her head with a feeling of deep sadness.

That may be the most depressing hour I've ever spent. I can't believe that Lewis Jefferson didn't even answer his letter. I wonder if he told Roger about it.

She opened the door of the van for Winston and headed for the lodge, knowing Gina would be waiting for her since she would be arriving late for the second day in a row.

CHAPTER TWENTY-THREE

"Gina, I am so sorry I'm late again. I'm beginning to feel like a lousy employer. This is the second day in a row I've made you wait. I promise it won't happen again."

"Don't worry, Liz. I saw Seth Williams this morning, and since he knows I'm working here, he told me you were helping him solve the murder of Gertie's step-brother. I imagine that's been on your mind as much as getting ready for the nightly dinners you prepare for the guests here at the lodge."

"Yes, that's true. I had several meetings this morning about it. Again, I'm really sorry about this. Give me just a minute, and we'll get started." She put her purse down on the counter and as she did, the clasp hit the edge of the countertop and sprang open, spilling the contests of her purse onto the floor.

"Liz, why don't you put your apron on and get the recipes for what we'll be serving tonight? I'll put all this stuff on the floor back in your purse," Gina said.

"Thanks. We're a little tight on time for what we'll be preparing for dinner. Give me one more minute. I want to go to the bathroom before we start. I'll be right back." When she returned she saw Gina peering intently at one of the photographs which had fallen out of her purse. "What is it, Gina?" Liz asked.

"It's none of my business, and if you don't want to tell me, I'll understand, but I'm curious why you have a picture of Olivia in your purse."

Liz looked over Gina's shoulder. She was holding the photograph the gallery owner had taken of the young woman who she had seen leaving the Jefferson Lumber property. "Do you know her?" Liz asked.

"Yes, very well. She's one of my best friends, although I don't see her as often as I did before she went to school at UC Berkeley."

"Please, tell me what you know about her. I've been trying to find someone who could identify the young woman in the photograph."

"Sure, I can help. I've known her forever. Her name is Olivia Jameson. She's my age, and we went all through school together. After we graduated from high school she went to Berkeley, and I stayed in Red Cedar, because my family couldn't afford for me to go away to college. Her mother had a heart attack a couple of months ago, and Olivia moved back home to take care of her mother and her two younger sisters. I've only talked to her a few times since then."

"Gina," Liz said, "do you have her telephone number? I'd really like to talk to her."

"It's on my cell phone contact list, but I left my phone at home. I usually carry it with me everywhere I go, but I needed to charge it, so I figured since I'd be working here this afternoon it would be a good time to do it."

"When you get home would you text me and let me know her number? I'll give her a call tomorrow. Actually, we really do need to get started on what we're going to serve for dinner tonight, so it's probably a good thing you don't have it, or I'd spend time calling her rather than doing what needs to be done. Let me write out a few instructions for you." A few minutes later she handed Gina a list and three recipes. She said, "I'll be working along with you. If you need any help, just ask."

The rest of the afternoon flew by as they completed the preparations for the evening's dinner. They'd just finished changing their clothes and lighting the candles when the first guest knocked on the door. A few minutes later Roger walked up the stairs, having used the outside door to their downstairs living quarters rather than entering through the main door of the lodge. He kissed Liz on the cheek and joined the other guests as they shared their day's spa experiences and enjoyed the wine and cheese Liz and Gina had set out for them.

*****

Later that evening as Gina was leaving, Liz reminded her to text her with Olivia's phone number. After she locked the front door Liz walked down the stairs to join Roger who had told her he needed to check a couple of his emails. She walked into his office and said, "Get everything done?"

"Yes. Sorry I didn't stay to help you and Gina clean up, but there were a couple of things I really needed to do. I'm finished now. What did you think of the meeting with Mark?"

"I liked him, and I think he's a wonderful man for what he's doing to help Brad. I had a long talk with Gertie, and then I went over to Brad's house and talked to him." She summed up her conversations with them and said, "Roger, I'm really troubled with something that has nothing to do with David's murder."

"What is it? You look depressed. Is everything okay with your kids? Is anything wrong?"

"The children are fine, but I think there's something really wrong with our world when a man goes to Afghanistan, defends our country, comes home, and gets cancer. To make matters worse, the cancer was probably caused by his being exposed to dangerous chemicals at work, so he writes a letter to the person in charge of the company where he works asking for help, and his letter is never answered."

"Why do I have a feeling this is about Jefferson Lumber Company?" Roger asked.

"Because it is, and I think it stinks," she said in a raised voice. She continued, "Did you know that Brad Cassidy wrote Lewis Jefferson a letter telling him he wouldn't sue Jefferson Lumber Company if Lewis would agree to pay his medical expenses when his insurance runs out?"

"No, Lewis never mentioned it to me. I wonder if he even got the letter. That doesn't sound like him."

"Well, if he did get it, and he ignored it, I'm putting him at the top of my 'Shameful People' list."

"I'd prefer to think he didn't get it. I'll ask him about it the next time I talk to him."

"I'd rather you didn't. My niggle's acting up. I have no idea why, but it seems to be telling me that you shouldn't say anything right now. Let me think about it for a bit."

"Out of deference to you I won't, but I'm just as curious about it as you are. I've always thought I was a pretty good judge of character. I'd hate to find out I made a big mistake in thinking he was one of the good guys."

"I haven't known you to be wrong too many times, so maybe it's all some big mistake. Anyway, I was able to find out the name of the young woman who was in the photograph that Joan Markham, the owner of the gallery, gave me."

"That's good news. How did you do that?"

"My purse came open when I was in the kitchen and everything fell out of it onto the floor. Gina happened to see the photograph of the young woman. She was curious why I would have a photo of one of her friends in my purse. I didn't tell her anything about it, just that I was trying to find out who she was. Gina didn't have the phone number for Olivia, that's her name, with her because it was on her cell phone, and she'd left it at home, so she could charge it. She's going to text me when she gets home, and I'll call Olivia tomorrow."

"Sounds like you're making some progress on the case. Have you talked to Seth recently?"

"No. I don't want to tell him anything, because he'd probably go to Gertie's and tell whoever is there everything he knows. Discretion is a term that doesn't seem to be in his vocabulary."

Roger laughed. "I certainly agree with you on that. I'm going to have to end this conversation and turn in for the night. I've got meetings all day tomorrow. Looks like more and more of the clients who used to go to our San Francisco office have decided my satellite office is a lot closer. If this keeps up I'm going to have to hire another secretary. Jessica's the best secretary I've ever worked with, but she can only do so much. She hasn't said anything, but I'm getting the distinct feeling she's a bit frustrated."

"I'll join you. Whatever sleuthing I do tomorrow had better be done in the morning, because I've been late getting back to the lodge the last two days, and Gina's had to sit in the kitchen doing nothing but waiting for me to return."

"And what you're not saying is that you're paying her to sit."

"You've got that right. I'm sure a business consultant would say that is a very bad business practice, and they'd probably be right," Liz said as she stood up to join him.

As Roger turned off the light in his study he said, "That might be, but I don't think you can put a financial value when it comes to helping people, and that's what you're doing. I, for one, think it's more important than anything defined by dollars and cents."

"Thanks, love, I needed to hear that," she said as they walked down the hall. Winston got on his dog bed in Roger's study, knowing he wasn't welcome in their bedroom.

CHAPTER TWENTY-FOUR

At 8:30 the next morning Liz called the number that Gina had sent to her the night before. After a few rings a soft voice answered the phone, "Hello."

"Is this Olivia Jameson?"

"Yes. Who's calling?"

"Olivia, my name is Liz Langley. A friend of yours, Gina Bartlett, works for me."

"Yes, I remember Gina telling me she was going to work for you the last time I saw her. What can I do for you?"

"I was wondering if you'd have time this morning to meet with me? I have something important I'd like to discuss with you."

"I just started working for Bart Stevenson at the Red Cedar Tribune. I do get a coffee break, and the office is right across from Gertie's Diner. I could meet you there at 10:00."

"That would be fine. I'll see you then. Bart's a friend of mine. Please tell him I said hello."

"Wait a minute, Mrs. Langley. Let me tell you what I look like."

"Olivia, I already know. I'll see you at Gertie's."

Liz spent some time going over paperwork Bertha had left for her. She wanted Liz to become familiar with the new employees she'd hired for the spa. At 9:45 Liz called to Winston, and the two of them got in her van. A few minutes later she found a parking place in front of Gertie's Diner and let Winston out of the car. He walked over to the front door of the diner, stopped, and looked back at Liz as if to say, "Hurry up. She always gives me leftovers. I love it here." Liz opened the door for him, and Gertie had Winston's harness in her hand by the time the door closed behind them.

"Saw ya' comin' thru the window. Two of my favorites. Here ya' go big guy, let's get this harness on ya'. Don't wanna be closed down, 'cuz I was nice to ya', but I gotta tell ya' I saw a chicken fried steak that was only half-eaten that has yer name all over it. I'll go get it fer ya' right now. Liz, take that booth over there."

Liz smiled as she watched the iconic octogenarian toddle to the kitchen on her five inch high heels. They settled into the booth, and a moment later a young waitress brought Liz water, Winston's chicken fried steak, and asked her if she was ready to order.

"Just coffee this morning, thanks. I'll be joined by another person," Liz said. Just then the door to the diner opened. Olivia walked in and started looking around. Liz waved to her and said to the waitress, "There she is now. If you can wait a moment, you can get her order as well."

Olivia walked over to the booth and Liz said, "Olivia, before we get started, what would you like? Thought we'd better order right away, because I know you're on a tight schedule, and I don't want Bart to get mad at me for keeping you."

Olivia looked at the waitress and said, "I'd like a cup of coffee with cream. Thanks." She sat down across from Liz as the waitress walked away from their table to get their coffee.

Liz smiled and began speaking, "Olivia, it's nice to meet you. I really appreciate you taking the time to see me. If you don't mind I have a couple of questions I'd like to ask you."

"Before we start, could you tell me how you know who I am?" Olivia asked.

"That's part of why I'm here." She told Olivia about how the gallery owner across the road from the Jefferson Lumber property had taken her photograph and given it to Liz. "A man was murdered by the name of David Sanders on the Jefferson Lumber Company property. He's Gertie's step-brother, and she's a friend of mine, so I'm helping with the investigation of the murder."

Olivia laughed and said, "I think she's everyone's friend."

"Yes, she's in a category all by herself. Anyway, David was with the Forestry Service and was murdered the afternoon your picture was taken. While the coroner can't tell the exact time he was murdered it was very close to the time you were seen there."

"Oh, no! I remember seeing something about it on television and now that you've told me, I do recall seeing a Forestry Service car in the parking lot when I left. That's awful."

"Olivia, why were you out at the Jefferson property? What were you doing there?"

"When I entered Berkeley I thought I wanted to teach English, but the more I learned about global warming and the effect it was going to have on the world, I realized that was a lot more important than studying poets and writers from hundreds of years ago. I changed my major to Environmental Sciences this year. I had a call from a friend of mine the day before I went out to the property. He taught the Introduction to Environment class I was taking. He told me that a Lotis Blue butterfly had been sighted on some lumber property in Red Cedar. He knew I lived in Red Cedar and asked if I could meet him, and he could follow me to the property, since he'd never been to Red Cedar."

"How well did you know him when you were at Berkeley, if you don't mind me asking?"

"I don't mind," Olivia said. "I didn't know him very well. He was a couple of years older than me and was working on his master's degree. That's why he was a teaching assistant. We had coffee a couple of times after class. We never dated or anything. We really were just friends."

"I wasn't implying otherwise. I'm just trying to understand your relationship with him."

"I understand, anyway, I met him that afternoon, and he followed me in his car to the Jefferson Lumber Company property. After we parked, I was curious and asked him about this butterfly. He told me about it being on the Endangered Species List, and that one had been spotted there."

"Did you see one?" Liz asked.

"No. Trace, that's his name, thought he saw one, and he went charging off into the woods to try and catch it. He'd even brought a butterfly net with him, if you can believe that. He ran farther and farther back into the forest. It was obvious he was pretty excited about the whole thing. He said if he could find the butterfly it would not only help him with getting his master's degree, it would probably assure him of being admitted into the doctoral program at Berkeley."

"Yes, I can sure see where that would have been a coup."

"Very much so."

"What happened after he chased the butterfly?"

"I never saw him again. I waited over fifteen minutes for him to come back, but he never did. Finally, I had to leave. You see, my mother had a heart attack a few months ago, and I'm helping take care of her and my sisters. As it turned out I probably could have stayed a little longer, because my sisters went to a friend's house that afternoon."

"What's the full name of the young man you were with that day?"

"His name is Trace Logan."

"Do you know where he lives?"

"I believe he said he grew up in Sacramento. I think he told me his father's a professor at the University of California at Davis. He's with the Environmental Sciences Department. It's probably not surprising that Trace wants to be a professor in Environmental Sciences."

"Olivia, I know your time is almost up. I want to show you a photograph that was taken about twenty minutes after the photograph of you was taken. Is the person in this photograph Trace Logan?"

"Yes, that's Trace." She took the photograph from Liz and held it in her hand while she studied it. Liz noticed that Olivia seemed to have a puzzled look on her face.

"Is something wrong?" Liz asked.

"It's this strange thing. I would have sworn that Trace had brown eyes. I thought I remembered them from when I was a student in his class. They were kind of puppy like, you know, all soft and warm, but in this photo and also when I saw him at the Jefferson property, his eyes were almost green. I told my mom about it, and she said maybe he wore a special type of contact lens which would explain it. I don't know, it's just kind of strange. Trace wasn't into fashion, so I find that kind of hard to believe, but it's the only explanation that makes sense, unless I was completely mistaken about his brown eye color."

"I have no idea why there might be a difference in his eye color. I, too, have heard that some people wear contact lens as a fashion accessory, but it seems to be more common among women rather than men. Anyway, I know you have to leave. I'll take care of the check, and I need to give this harness my dog is wearing back to Gertie."

"I wondered about that. I've never seen a dog in here before, and you don't look like you need a therapy dog."

"Don't tell anyone, but Gertie likes Winston. She bought a harness with the words "Therapy Dog" on it for him at a garage sale, so he can come in here with me. Actually, I think it's kind of cute, and it stops people from complaining about a dog being in a restaurant. Anyway, if you find something out about Trace or remember anything else that might be related to the murder, I'd like to know."

"If I hear from him I'll let you know. Be sure and tell Gina hi for me. Tell her I'll call her as soon as my mom gets better, and I have a little more time for myself."

"I will and good luck with your new job. Don't give up on getting your college degree. You can think of this time you're spending with your mother as a little hiccup."

"I don't know, I think it's more of a burp," she said laughing as she scooted out of the booth.

CHAPTER TWENTY-FIVE

Liz left the diner feeling unsettled. Her niggle was clamoring for attention, and she wasn't sure about what. The more she thought about her conversation with Olivia and the color of Trace's eyes, something didn't seem right. Olivia seemed like a highly intelligent young woman. The fact she would leave college to help her family and was managing to take care of her mother and two sisters, plus hold a job, said a lot for the young woman.

I need to call Sean and see if he can come up with anything on Trace. Should have called him earlier. He's been a huge help to me on other cases. How lucky am that I my husband's law firm probably has the best private investigator probably on the West Coast. He can find things out that no one else can. Definitely can use his help about now.

As soon as she and Winston got back to the lodge she sat down and called Sean. A moment later she heard, "Liz, how are you? I haven't talked to you in a long time. Now that Roger opened the office in Red Cedar, I talk to him once in a while, but it's not like it was when he worked here at the San Francisco office. I'm assuming you'd like my help on something. What can I do for you?"

She told him about the case she was working on and then began to tell him why she'd called. "Would you see if you can find out about a young man named Trace Logan? He's a master's degree student in Environmental Sciences at UC Berkeley and is a teaching assistant there. He's about 6'0" tall and has brown hair. From the photograph I have he doesn't look like he's overweight or underweight, just average."

"You can stop there, Liz. I know you have the ability to scan a photograph and send it to me. You've done it before. Just send his photo to me, and I'll take it from there. Anything else I should know?"

"His father's a professor at UC Davis, and Trace grew up in Sacramento. Since his father teaches so close to Sacramento, I imagine his father still lives there. I don't know about his mother. Oh, there is one thing that's odd." Liz told him about Olivia and the confusion over the color of Trace's eyes.

"Liz, you caught me at a really good time. I finished up a report a few minutes ago, and I have a meeting with one of the partners in a couple of hours, so I can get right on this. I'll call you when I know something."

"Thanks, Sean. You can bill Roger for this and tell him it's about his Jefferson Lumber Company client," she said smiling.

"Liz, you've listened to my lady friend problems a few times, and I appreciate it. As the old saying goes, this one is on the house."

"Thanks, Sean."

She heard footsteps coming down the hall and a moment later Bertha walked into the room carrying a number of files. "Did you have a chance to check out the applications of the people I hired? I know you trust my judgment, but I like you to know what I'm doing."

"Bertha, you're absolutely right. I trust your judgment completely, and it looks like you did a great job by hiring that group. At some point we're either going to have to build more cottages or stop hiring people. What percent of the spa appointments are from people who aren't staying here?"

"About seventy-five percent. Most of them are from San Francisco or people staying at a couple of the bed and breakfasts in town or in nearby towns. I don't think we need to build any more cottages, but if this keeps up we may have to expand the spa. I brought you some mock-ups of ads I'd like to run in a few papers and believe it or not, even on Facebook. The spa already has a page on it, and we get a lot of customers from that source. Thought we ought to up the ante, so to speak, and increase our presence on Facebook."

"I've got a little time right now," Liz said, taking the files from Bertha. "I'll let you know what I think, but I doubt I'll be able to improve on what you've come up with."

"I don't know about that. See you later," she said taking the personnel applications off of Liz's desk.

*****

Liz immersed herself in the ads Bertha had prepared and hoped that the cost of the ads would be offset by bringing in new customers. The ringing of her phone jolted her out of her thoughts. She looked at the screen and saw that the call was from Sean.

"Good grief, Sean. That was fast."

"Well, when you're only twenty-two years old, you don't have much of a past, so there's not that much to discover about the young man named Trace Logan, however, I did find the answer to the difference in eye colors. Trace has an identical twin. I did a little research, and even though they're identical twins, it's possible for their eye color to be different. From what you told me I think Trace probably is on the brown end of the hazel spectrum, and his brother, whose name is Kyle, is on the green end of the spectrum. That takes care of the eye color confusion.

"I didn't find much out about Trace other than what you told me, at least nothing that will probably help you. I took the liberty of researching his brother, and he's a different story. Kyle has been very active in almost every environmental battle in California for the last five years. He works for the California Forestry Service and ..."

He heard Liz's sharp intake of breath. "Liz, what's wrong?"

"I find that frightening. I mean David Sanders, the man who was murdered, was employed by the Forestry Service, and now you're telling me that Kyle is as well. Was he with the office in Sacramento?"

"Yes. He's also been very involved in all different types of efforts to save endangered species. One you've probably heard about in the local media is a little fish found in the waters near Sacramento called the Delta Smelt. It's on the Endangered Species List, and Kyle has been active in seeking protection for it. He was part of the group that successfully stopped the pumping of water from Northern California to Southern California. It's caused a huge uproar in the farming communities of the Central Valley."

"Oh, dear," Liz said, involuntarily.

"Why the 'oh dear'?" Sean asked.

"I don't like what I'm thinking. Sean, thanks for your help. I think I need to tell Roger what I've found out. He's always a good sounding board."

"Do me a favor, Liz. I know you have a tendency sometimes to go off half-cocked. If you can't get ahold of Roger, I'll say it for him. Don't do anything that could be dangerous. Hear me?"

"Yes, I promise I won't. Thanks again. I'll talk to you soon."

As she was calling Roger, her phone buzzed. She switched to the incoming call and answered it. "This is Liz Langley."

"Liz, I'm glad I got ahold of you. This is Joan Markham with the Markham Art Gallery."

"Joan, how nice to hear from you. I hope this is about making a reservation here at the spa."

"Actually, it's not. I told you about my compulsion to take photographs, and I thought you should know about what I've seen recently. Every day for the last few days I've seen the young man who was in the photograph I gave you go onto the Jefferson Lumber property that's across the road from my gallery. He always had a butterfly net with him, so I figured he'd spotted some rare type of butterfly on the Jefferson property, but I did think it was a little odd."

"I think it's odd, too, and with what I just found out only minutes ago, I think it's even odder."

"I'd like to hear what you have to say, but let me finish telling you about him. He came back this afternoon, just a few minutes ago, and what's of concern to me is that he was carrying a large bag from the hardware store. I shop there, so I recognized the name on the bag. I wouldn't be concerned except I recently saw a show on TV about something called tree spiking. It talked about how people who didn't want trees to be cut down drove long heavy spikes into the trees. Then when the property owner starts to harvest the trees the chainsaw hits the steel spike and the saw literally explodes. It often results in people being hurt. Sometimes it's a lumberjack, and other times it's someone at the sawmill who gets injured or even killed."

"I'd forgotten about the practice of tree spiking. I remember seeing something awhile ago regarding it on some science show my husband was watching. Apparently the practice of spiking trees is a terribly dangerous and malicious thing to do. Do you think there's some relationship between tree spiking and the young man you saw going into the forest carrying a bag from the hardware store?"

"I have no idea, but I can tell you this. The bag appeared to be quite heavy, and he was having trouble holding it in one hand because he was carrying a small sledge hammer in his other hand. It just seemed very strange to me, and I thought you might want to know about it. I would have called the police, but I was afraid I'd get that ignorant chief of police. I met him once and long ago decided if

I ever had a problem, he'd be the last person I'd call."

"Is the young man still in the forest?"

"Yes. Why?"

"I'd like to talk to him. I'm going to go over there right now. I'll let you know what I find out."

She quickly wrote out instructions for Gina and put the recipes for the evening's dinner on the kitchen counter. She ended her note by saying she was going to check out something on the Sanders case at the scene of the crime, and she'd be back in time for dinner.

"Winston, time to go for a ride," she said, opening the door of her van. *Darn, I better take my gun with me. If Roger finds it at home I'll never hear the end of it.* Liz ran back to where she'd put it in the drawer of her desk, quickly slipped the gun into her jacket pocket, and hurried back to her van.

CHAPTER TWENTY-SIX

Liz pulled into the parking lot adjacent to the Jefferson Lumber Company property and noticed several other cars in the lot. She hadn't thought to ask Sean what kind of a car Kyle drove. She parked her van and looked around. It was an eerily peaceful crime scene. Yellow tape was still up, and she didn't hear the sound of trees being cut down. She got out of her van, motioned for Winston to follow her, and made sure her pistol was in her pocket. She had no idea where Kyle was or if he was even in the forest. The farther she walked into it, the darker it got. Even though it was not yet dusk, she wished she'd thought to bring a flashlight. She stopped and cocked her head. She thought she heard the sound of a hammer in the distance.

She motioned for Winston to stay behind her as she carefully walked towards the direction from which she thought she'd heard the hammering sounds. Liz was glad she'd put on the Croc shoes that chefs wore when they were cooking. Not only did they help her when she stood for long periods of time in the kitchen, but in the forest they kept her footsteps silent. Ahead of her, in the dim light, she could just barely make out the form of a man. He was swinging a sledgehammer and appeared to be driving metal spikes into trees. She stepped behind a large tree and motioned for Winston to join her.

There were no sounds coming from the birds and animals that lived in the forest, and she thought that was odd. She wondered if the animals that were normally quite active sensed the man she was watching had killed someone, and therefore their lives might also be in jeopardy. On the drive to the parking lot the pieces of the puzzle had tumbled together in her mind, and Liz was certain that Kyle Logan was the person who had murdered David Sanders. The motive probably made perfect sense to Kyle. He was worried David would find the Lotis Blue butterfly and destroy it, so there wouldn't be any evidence that the endangered blue butterfly existed. If no evidence existed the lumber company could continue to fell the trees, which of course would destroy the butterfly's sole remaining habitat. Without its habitat the butterfly would be unable to live and would truly become extinct. Kyle probably felt he was doing a great service for any surviving Lotis Blue butterflies.

Liz moved forward from tree to tree, and as she got closer to Kyle she saw he was in fact hammering three to four long spikes into mature trees in a systematical manner. There was no doubt about the purpose of his actions. Someone either at the site or at the sawmill was going to be injured or killed by his tree spiking actions. He probably hoped that once that happened the trees in the area would stop being felled, and the butterfly's habitat would be saved.

Kyle was so intent on what he was doing he was oblivious to Liz who now stood no more than ten feet from him. She took the gun from her pocket and said, "Kyle, drop your hammer…" He instantly swung around and threw the sledgehammer at her. It missed her head by inches, but the handle grazed her arm and caused her to drop her gun. Sensing Liz was in danger, Winston growled and attacked Kyle, slamming his full weight into him and pushing Kyle to the ground. The ninety-five pound dog stood over Kyle and pinned him to the ground, at the same time snapping and snarling at him while he was only inches from Kyle's face. Liz stood slightly back from him and retrieved her gun from where it had fallen on the ground.

"Kyle, I want you to tell me the truth, or I'm going to give the dog a command that will result in some serious pain for you. I also have my gun aimed at you, and I'm a crack shot. You killed David Sanders, didn't you?"

She heard a muffled voice. "Kyle, speak up. I can't hear what you're saying."

"Yes I did," he practically shouted as he struggled in vain to get away from Winston. "I knew he was going to do something to make sure no one knew the Lotis Blue butterfly was ever here. I overheard him talking on the phone one night. He thought everyone in the office had gone home. He told whoever it was he was talking to that he'd make sure no endangered species were ever found on the Jefferson Lumber Company property. I don't know if he was getting money for doing that, but I'll bet he was."

"Kyle, you pretended you were Trace. How did you know Olivia's phone number and where she lived?"

"I remembered Trace said something when he came home from college one time about becoming friends with a girl from Red Cedar. When I found out the Lotis Blue butterfly had been sighted on some lumber property in Red Cedar, all I had to do was hack into his computer and get her phone number. He calls himself an environmentalist, but he's one in name only. All he wants to do is preserve and protect the natural resources of California. In this case, things like trees, so big corporation can strip them bare and leave future generations of Californians with nothing. I'm the one who truly helps save the environment and all the rare and endangered plants and animals in it that are threatened with extinction. Anyway, there's no one around to hear our conversation, and I'll never admit to anyone what I just said. I want to know how you think you're going to get me to go anywhere. There's just you and this dumb dog. Looks like you've got yourself a big problem."

"It's not her problem, friend," a voice said from behind Liz. "It's yours, and I recorded your whole conversation. I've spent most of my life in courts of law, and it's been my experience that this type of a confession will stand up and make for an easy conviction on a charge of murder to say nothing of a federal offense for tree spiking. From this moment on, I don't think you need to worry about the environment. The only environment you're going to be seeing is the inside of a prison cell for a long, long time, if not the rest of your life.

"Roger, I've never been so glad to see someone in my life!" Liz exclaimed, "but why are you here? How did you find me?"

"Let me call Seth, Liz, and then I'll fill you in. Don't move," he said to Kyle as he took his phone out of his pocket and pressed in Seth's phone number, all the while keeping his gun aimed at Kyle. "Friend, I've used this before, and I'll use it now if I have to, so don't give me a reason to."

A few moments later Liz heard Seth's voice coming from Roger's phone which he'd put on speaker. "Roger, you caught me jes' as I was fillin' out some more reports on them speedin' tickets I gave out today. I think maybe I done gone and broke my one day record. Boy, howdy, were them out-of-towners puttin' the pedal to the metal today. Musta' caught me nearly fifty of 'em. Anyway, what can I do fer ya' and how's that gorgeous wife of yours doin? Ain't talked to her in awhile."

"You'll be talking to her real soon, Seth. She caught David's killer. The case is solved. I need you to come out here to where David was killed and bring your deputy. Think you're going to be filling out even more papers."

"Oh man, jes' when I thought I was near finished. Okay, guess I gotta do my chief thing. I'll be out there shortly."

"Roger, while we're waiting for Seth please tell me how you happened to find me. I mean this location is a little more than off the beaten path. In fact it's in the middle of nowhere in a dense forest."

"Sean called me and was worried you were going to do something rash with the information he'd given you. He's pretty good at reading people, and he thought I ought to know what he'd found out. I called your cell phone, but you didn't answer, so I called the lodge. Gina answered and told me you weren't there, but you'd left a note for her. She read it to me, and I became concerned. I got in my car and when I started driving out I remembered what you told me about the gallery owner. I called her, and she told me about Kyle, the heavy sack from the hardware store, her suspicion that Kyle might be engaging in an act of tree spiking, and finally that you'd just pulled into the parking lot. I was able to get here a few minutes later. I heard the sound of a hammer and went in that direction. That's about it."

"Oh, thank you, Roger," Liz said in a ragged voice. "I didn't know how I was going to get him out of here, and I'm so glad you taped his confession. I was worried it would be my word against his and since no one saw him, and the murder weapon hasn't been found…"

She cocked her head at the sound of a police siren approaching. They heard Seth yelling, "Liz, Roger, where are ya'? Can't see hardly nuthin'. It's darker than a bat's cave back here in this forest."

"We're over here, Seth," Roger yelled. A few minutes later the fat police chief and his deputy came crashing through the forest. "Glad I got here in time. We'll take it from here. Probably need some professionals 'bout now," he said self-importantly. "Liz, call that dog off'n him."

"Winston, stand down. Come. That's a good boy. Might have to stop by Gertie's for a special treat for you. Oh Roger, that reminds me. Can I have your phone? I need to call Gina. She's probably a nervous wreck by now."

"Gina, it's Liz. I'm sorry I'm not there. I'll explain everything when I get to the lodge. You're doing fine and enjoying it? I don't need to hurry? Are you sure? Well, great. I knew you could do it. I'll be there in a little while. It sounds like you have everything under control, so if I'm not there, enjoy!"

She turned to Roger. "Hiring her was one of the best things I ever did. She said everything's been done, and all she's doing is waiting for the first of the guests to arrive."

"Time to go home, sweetheart," Roger said. "We can call Gertie and everyone and tell them what's happened when we get back to the lodge. We're both a mess and need to change clothes before we greet your guests, so let's go in by the downstairs side door."

"Seth, I've got spa guests coming momentarily," Liz said "Okay with you if I go to your office tomorrow to give a statement?"

"Sure, darlin'. Whatever. Gonna have my hands full tonight with all these reports. We'll get him locked up in the cell like pronto. What's his name?"

"His name is Kyle Logan. If you need any other information tonight, give me a call."

"Liz, if you're up to driving, I'll meet you at the lodge. Winston, you go with her," Roger said. He opened the van's door for both of them and shook his head. "Liz, see these grey hairs on my temples. As Seth would say, 'darlin', I think that's what he calls you, they're multiplying like crazy because of you."

"And you wouldn't have it any other way, would you?"

CHAPTER TWENTY-SEVEN

Liz drove up the lane leading to the lodge with Winston at her side, relieved that the killer had been caught and things could return to normal. She felt badly about leaving Gina alone to deal with tonight's dinner, but from the candles shining through the windows of the lodge, and the people she could see seated at the table smiling and laughing, it appeared that Gina was able to handle things very easily on her own.

She entered the lodge through the kitchen side door and found Gina putting the last touches on the main course she was getting ready to serve. "I am so sorry for abandoning you," Liz said, "but I have a pretty good excuse. We caught the murderer we've been looking for. By the time I waited for Seth and talked to him and his deputy, I knew I wouldn't make it back here in time for dinner, but you seem to have handled everything beautifully. Since you're doing so well, I really need to call a couple of people and tell them what's happened. Can you take care of the rest of the meal by yourself?"

"Of course. This is fun, and I've discovered I can do it all by myself. Actually I'm glad it happened this way, because I don't think I would have ever felt ready to do it on my own. Take your time and do what you need to do."

Liz went downstairs and joined Roger. "Liz, I'm going to pass on being with the guests tonight. I hope you don't mind, but I left work in such a hurry there were a couple of things I didn't get around to finishing. I really need to take care of them now."

"That's fine, Roger. Gina's doing so well I don't need to be there either, and I want to call Gertie and a couple of other people." She walked into her office, Winston by her side. The dog had always been protective of her, but after today, she sensed he was taking it to a whole new level.

*****

The first person on Liz's list of people she wanted to call was Gertie. She knew how happy Gertie would be that the hunt for her step-brother's killer was over. She pressed Gertie's number into her phone and a moment later heard Gertie's voice. "Hey, honey, what's so important ya' need to call me at night?"

"Gertie, I wanted you to be the first to know that we found out who murdered David, and he's in jail at this minute. Here's what happened." Liz told how she had determined Kyle was the killer and what had taken place.

"Well, I'll be durned, so it weren't George. Woulda' bet everything on that horse and then not been able to cash that ticket. Bet yer' handsome husband weren't too happy 'bout the part ya' played in catchin' the killer."

"You've got that right. I'm going to have to do some serious cooking to make up for not letting him know where I was going. By the way, I never told you about how I made the decision to let Ruby Myers stay in David's apartment until the killer was caught. She was afraid of her husband and probably with good cause. She was pretty sure he'd followed her to the Jefferson property and had seen David's car in the lot. As I told you, I thought if there was any chance that the killer was interested in you because you were David's step-sister, that the less you knew the better it was for you."

"No prob. Matter of fact, might be a good idea for her to stay there for awhile. Might make it real clear to George that while he's doing better with controlling his anger, he still needs to do a little more work in that area, like maybe seeing the shrink a lot more. Whaddya' think?"

"Gertie, I think that's very generous of you. I'll give Ruby a call. I'm sure she's terrified. I've talked to her a couple of times, but I really didn't have much to tell her. I'll call her now."

"Okay. Say ya' spoke to me, and I said she can stay there as long as she wants. I'm David's next of kin, so guess I'll be inheritin' whatever he has, and that includes the apartment. Think you tol' me Mitch Stevenson over at the Forestry Service office in Sacramento was takin' care of it. Ya' plannin' on callin' him?"

"Yes. I'll call Ruby, and then I'll call him. I probably also should call George. I'll give you a call tomorrow and let you know what happens. Since you have to be at the diner really early, it's probably getting near your bedtime."

"That it is, honey. Think I'll jes' say nitey-nite and head for bed now, but want ya' to know that I'll be sleepin' a lot better tonight than I have been. Thanks, Liz."

"Happy I could do something for one of my favorite diner owners, although I might just ask for a hamburger and malt on the house next time I come to the diner."

"Honey, consider it done! Plus I might jes' be able to rustle up a little somethin' fer that big dog."

*****

"Ruby, it's Liz Langley. I just wanted to call and let you know we caught the person that murdered David Sanders."

"I'm afraid to ask if it was George," she said.

"No. George had nothing to do with it. I think he was following you to see if you were going to meet David. The killer was a man by the name of Kyle Logan, and his motive was to protect an endangered butterfly called the Lotis Blue butterfly. Evidently the young man thought David might locate it and not make it public so timber harvesting could continue on the site. Apparently he thought David might be less than honest when it came to protecting an endangered species."

"I don't know where he got that idea. I certainly never saw that side of David."

"Well," Liz said, "I guess we'll never know. I just spoke with Gertie. She was convinced George was the murderer. I told her how afraid of him you were, and she suggested you stay in David's apartment until George gets more professional help. The thought occurs to me that maybe you could talk to Mitch about getting back your old job with the Forestry Service now that David's no longer there."

"That's a wonderful idea. I really love George, but I don't want to live the rest of my life in fear of my husband. If he could get more help and was willing to commit to getting a handle on his anger, I'd go back to him, but right now I can't. Do you understand?" she asked as she started to cry.

"Ruby, you've been through a lot the last few days. Give yourself a little time and then trust your instincts. You seem to be a very sensible person, and there's a good chance that George will be able to successfully deal with his anger. A lot of other people have problems, and they're able to get past them. I'm sure he can, too."

"Liz, thank you for everything. I'll give Mitch a call tomorrow morning and see if he'll take me back until I sort everything out. One last thing. Have you talked to George?"

"No. I still have to call him."

"I'd like to call him if you don't mind. I can tell him I love him, and I want to reconcile with him, but he needs to get a lot more help with his anger issues before I do that. I think it might be better if it came from me."

"I think that's a wonderful idea, Ruby, however I do want to caution you about telling him exactly where you're living until you know for sure he's getting some help. Maybe he could give his doctor permission to tell you the status of how he's doing. I know there's something about doctors not being able to release information unless the patient consents to it. If he would agree to it, you could monitor his progress through the doctor, and the two of you could decide when it would be appropriate for you to return."

"I will. Again, thanks for calling."

"The next person on my list is Mitch. I'll mention that you'll be calling him. Good night."

*****

"Mitch, this is Liz Langley. I'm sorry to bother you at home, but a few things have happened, and I promised I'd let you know when I knew anything."

"We must be on the same wavelength, Liz. I was just getting ready to call you. Since you called, you go first."

She told him everything that had happened, and that Ruby would be calling him in the morning.

"Liz, it turns out none of this needed to happen."

"What are you talking about?" she asked.

"Something didn't seem right to me about the Lotis Blue butterfly sighting. I did some research on the two people who sent the letter about the sighting and the photograph they said they took of it. The photograph was what bothered me. I'm an environmentalist at heart, and I watch every science and nature program that's on television. I also subscribe to a number of magazines on the subject. When I closely examined the letter I knew I'd seen that photograph before. I got out all of my old magazine issues, because I was sure it was something I'd seen in the last two years. It's a long story, but my wife made me pack up a bunch of them, and anyway, I was able to locate the photo in one of the magazines. It was a perfect match."

"You're kidding. Was there even a sighting of a Lotis Blue butterfly?"

"That's what I'm getting to. I met with the two people who sent the letter and showed them the photograph that was in the magazine and the one they had sent to my office. I told them I knew they had simply copied the photograph in the magazine and used it in the letter and that there had never been a sighting of a Lotis Blue butterfly on the Jefferson property. They finally admitted they'd done it in an attempt to stop the trees on the Jefferson property from being logged. Kyle must have seen the letter, and that's why he went to the site after he learned David was going to investigate the sighting. I sent David there based on the letter which it turns out was completely fraudulent. I never should have sent him there. It's my fault for immediately assuming that there had been a sighting. I should have been more diligent. I don't know if I can ever forgive myself."

"You can't blame yourself, Mitch. When you receive information about a threat to an endangered species, it's your responsibility to investigate. That's why you sent David to the site. Any other manager in your position would have sent someone out too. You didn't do anything wrong. Kyle Logan was the one who did something horribly wrong and something that is affecting a lot of lives, like Ruby Myers." She told him about the conversation she'd just had with Ruby, and how she would be calling Mitch in the morning.

"Mitch, I'm curious about something. Kyle hinted that David might be on the take from some organizations that were not as environmentally friendly as you seem to be. Do you know anything about that? I suppose it doesn't matter now, but I'm curious."

There was a long silence on the other end of the phone and then Mitch spoke, "He could have been. I've heard rumors, but I never found any firm evidence. It wouldn't be the first time something like that has happened. I was approached years ago and told I could make some easy money by not reporting sightings of anything that was on the Endangered Species List because of the problems the sightings caused to business interests. I said no, but that doesn't mean there weren't other people getting money for not reporting sightings."

"So what you're saying is we'll never know what David would have done if he had discovered the Lotis Blue butterfly on the Jefferson property. He may have reported it, or he may have decided to say that nothing was found."

"Yes. We'll never know, and it's a moot point now because the whole thing was a hoax. What a tragic turn of events."

"Yes and no. People die, people go to prison, and some people turn their lives around because of a tragedy. I'm hopeful this will result in Ruby's husband being the success in this tragedy and learning to overcome his anger issues. This whole thing might result in a marriage being saved."

"Liz, let me ask you something. How do you view the world? Do you see it as a glass half-full or a glass half-empty?"

She quickly answered, "Half-full, of course. Is there even a choice?"

"No, I suppose not."

"I have a question for you, Mitch. I assume there will be no more attempts to stop the timber harvesting activities on the Jefferson property."

"That's true. That property will no longer be under any scrutiny by the Forestry Service. Would you like me to call the owner of the lumber company and tell him?"

"No, let me take care of it. While we were talking I've come up with an idea that just might result in a good thing happening as a consequence of David's tragic death. I'll take care of it. It's been a long day, and I'm tired. Thanks for everything, Mitch. Good night."

She walked into Roger's office and said, "Roger, I'd like to meet with Lewis Jefferson tomorrow. Could you set up a meeting in your office some time before 2:00? I've been lucky with Gina today, but if I'm a no-show tomorrow, I could be looking at having to hire a new sous-chef."

"Want to tell me what this is about? After all, Lewis is my client."

"No counsellor. Just trust me. I think you'll be happy with the outcome."

CHAPTER TWENTY-EIGHT

Roger called Liz after he got to his office and said, "I've set up a meeting for 11:00 this morning with Lewis. He's very curious. I told him I had no idea why you wanted to meet with him. Is there anything I should know before he comes in?"

"No, just trust me. I'll see you at 11:00."

Promptly at 11:00 she walked into Roger's office accompanied by Winston. She recognized Lewis Jefferson from the day at the logging site when David's body had been discovered. Roger's secretary said, "Mrs. Langley, Mr. Jefferson, Roger told me to tell you to please go into his office when both of you were here."

Liz and Lewis sat in the client chairs in Roger's law office, Roger across the desk from them, and Winston next to Liz's feet. Both of the men looked expectantly at Liz.

"Roger, Lewis, thank you for agreeing to meet with me. Lewis, I have some very good news for you, but first I want to talk to you about a situation that has come to my attention."

He spread his hands. "Mrs. Langley," he began.

"Please, call me Liz."

"All right, Liz. I'm completely in the dark here. I'm glad you have good news. These days we can all use some good news, but what is the situation you're referring to?"

"You have an employee by the name of Brad Cassidy who has developed cancer. There is some talk that it was caused because he was improperly exposed to formaldehyde at your plywood plant. Your employees are well aware of this situation, and if jobs in the lumber industry weren't so hard to come by, a number of them would have left because of it. The morale at your company is not good at the moment."

"How do you know about that? Did Roger tell you that?" he asked, glaring at Roger.

"No, one of your employees told me how bad the morale is. What I'm proposing to you is a way to fix your company's morale and also put you in a very favorable light with your employees."

"I'm certainly willing to listen, but I can't guarantee you I'll do anything."

"I understand. Brad wrote you a letter after he was diagnosed with cancer a couple of months ago. In the letter he said he wouldn't sue your company, because he didn't want his friends to be out of jobs and he was afraid if he won a large lawsuit and was awarded a large settlement it might bankrupt the company even though his doctor strongly urged him to do so. In his letter he asked that your company pay his medical bills when his insurance runs out. He told me he never heard from you."

"The reason he never heard from me is because I never received a letter from him. I was told that one of our employees had gotten cancer, but I assumed he was doing all right, since I hadn't heard from him or been sued."

"No, he is definitely not doing well. As a matter of fact the family can barely make ends meet. His wife is working two jobs, and Brad is worried about what will happen to them if he lives and can't work or worse yet, what will happen to them if he dies. He has many friends in your company. They pass a hat around weekly after they get their paychecks, and one of the employees takes the money they raise and puts an envelope with the money in it in Brad's mail box, because they know Brad would never take the money if he knew it was coming from them."

"What are you suggesting, Liz?"

"I was able to find the man who murdered David Sanders on your property. I have been in contact with the head of the Forestry Service in Sacramento, and he discovered that the Lotis Blue butterfly sighting was a hoax aimed at shutting down the harvesting of trees on your property by some overzealous environmentalists."

"What does that have to do with Brad?"

"I've been able to ensure that logging can now resume on your property. In other words, the yellow tape will now come down, because the crime has been solved, and since now there is no threat of logging being held up for a long time, perhaps years, I have a favor to ask of you."

"What is it, Liz?" Roger asked, not sure where she was headed. This was the first he'd heard of the blue butterfly hoax.

"Lewis, I think it would be in the best interests of your company for you to pay the medical expenses of Brad Cassidy as well as give him a cash settlement for his suffering. I'm sure Roger can draw a document up, so that neither he nor his family would be able to sue you or your company in the future no matter what happens with his health situation. You could post something in a company newsletter that you were helping the family and would hope that others would take time to drop him a healing note or some such thing. You'd come out looking like a prince, you'd prevent a lawsuit, and you'd do wonders for the morale of your workers. What do you say?"

He was quiet for several long moments, and then he spoke, "I had some problems with a couple of temporary secretaries about the time he must have sent me the letter you're referring to. It probably got lost in the shuffle. I've been concerned that my manager might not have been as diligent as he should have been in making sure there weren't problems with the formaldehyde used at the plywood plant. What you're presenting is a way for me to get out of a potentially messy situation as well as look good in the eyes of my employees." He turned to Roger and said, "Please draw up the necessary papers."

"Thank you, Lewis. You're doing the right thing. I do have one more request," she said.

Roger and Lewis exchanged glances as if to say "What now?"

"Yes, what is it?" Lewis asked.

"I'd like to be the one to tell Brad. Would that be all right with you?"

"Considering what you've done for my company, I would be more than happy to grant that request."

Liz stood up and smiled at Roger. "Winston and I are going home now. I need to make a phone call."

*****

"Brad," she said an hour later, "It's Liz Langley. I have some very good news for you…" Winston was lying at her feet listening to the conversation. He looked up at her and she could swear he winked at her.

EPILOGUE

Several months have passed since Liz determined that Kyle Logan was responsible for the murder of David Sanders. The long winter months on the North Coast of California with one storm after another crashing into the coast from the north had finally given way to spring.

The first day of spring was a beautiful warm day in Red Cedar. The sun was shining brightly, birds were singing, and the bulbs residents had planted in their front yards the previous fall were starting to bloom in a flowery show of color.

Roger and Liz Langley: On the first day of spring Liz was tending to some last minute arrangements for the new group of guests that would be checking into the cottages later in the day at the Red Cedar Spa and Lodge. Roger was preparing for a trial scheduled to start the next day.

Winston and Brandy Boy: The two dogs were sleeping on the front porch of the lodge enjoying the warm sunshine, something that had eluded them for the past few months. Both kept one ear cocked hoping to hear a sound from the kitchen that might mean they could enjoy some leftovers from the previous night's dinner at the lodge.

Ruby and George Myers: With an approval from George's doctor, Ruby had reconciled with George who seemed to have conquered his anger issues and now they were just a bad memory.

Gertie: Like almost every other day of the year, the first day of spring at Gertie's Diner was filled with hungry customers. The amazing octogenarian who tottered around on five inch high stilettos and who seemed to be living in a bygone era was busy serving up her famous hamburgers and malts, while at the same time keeping up on all the latest town gossip.

Seth Williams: The fat police chief, after having breakfast at Gertie's and spilling some of his fried eggs on the front of his uniform shirt as was his usual practice, was patiently sitting in his police car hidden behind a row of bushes, waiting for the next unsuspecting out-of-towner to come speeding through the speed trap he had conveniently constructed on the outskirts of town.

Lewis Jefferson: The owner of Jefferson Lumber Company was glad spring had finally arrived. With the rainy winter weather now a distant memory, he would be able to increase the rate of timber harvesting on the company's timber properties. Employee morale had never been better after he announced that the company would assume full responsibility for Brad Cassidy's cancer treatment. Additionally, the company and Brad had entered into a financial settlement to resolve Brad's voiced claim of misconduct concerning the use of formaldehyde at the company's plywood plant. Both parties were satisfied with the terms of the settlement, especially Brad, who thought the settlement was extremely generous.

Brad Cassidy: Life was much better for the Cassidy family as they no longer had to worry about their financial future after receiving the generous settlement from Jefferson Lumber Company. There was even a hint from Brad's doctors that his cancer might be in remission. A few more tests were going to be needed to confirm their suspicions.

Olivia Jameson: At the urging of her mother, she applied for a scholarship at UC Berkeley and it was granted. She's scheduled to resume her studies at the university in the fall.

Trace Logan: He's finishing up his master's degree and has been accepted as a doctoral candidate in the Environmental Studies program at UC Berkeley. When he called Olivia to apologize for his brother putting her in danger, one thing led to another, and they both are very much looking forward to spending some time together at Berkeley.

Kyle Logan: Although his attorney tried on repeated occasions to convince him to take the District Attorney's plea bargain offer, he refused. He feels that he is the savior of endangered species and if lives like his have to be sacrificed for those species, so be it. At the present time he's in jail awaiting his trial.

The Lotis Blue Butterfly: On this beautiful first day of spring, in a remote and rugged coastal bog located ten miles north of Red Cedar, a small but ever so beautiful little butterfly rides the ocean wind currents as it flits from bush to bush in the bog. With bright blue colored wings that measure only one inch from tip to tip, it looks exactly like the butterfly featured in the magazine Mitch Stevenson had shown Liz several months earlier. This particular butterfly is a female, and it delicately lands on a leafy green bush that's shining brightly in the warm morning sun. She lingers on the bush for several minutes, warming her body in the sunlight. After a minute or two she flaps her tiny wings, lifts herself into the air, and drifts away in the wind towards other areas of the bog, never to be seen again.

Several weeks later, on the same bush where the little blue butterfly had paused for a few minutes on the first day of spring, several small bluish colored caterpillars, no larger than a grain of rice, could be seen munching on the green leaves of the bush where the little blue butterfly had paused several weeks earlier.

And so the cycle of life continues, despite the activities of men and their machines.

RECIPES

CATFISH PASTA PRIMAVERA

Ingredients

12 oz. fettuccine

½ small red pepper, cut into strips (I usually quarter them, take out the white membrane and the seeds with a knife and put them in a stack. Think it makes cutting them easier. I do the same for the yellow pepper.)

½ small yellow pepper, cut into strips

4 oz. pea pods, trimmed (By trimming, I mean to cut the end off and then pull off the tough string that runs along the length of the pod. You might get lucky and find the store has already done it for you.)

6 green onion, chopped in thin slices

2 tbsp. chopped shallots (Remember to remove the outer papery covering.)

¼ cup butter (An easy way to measure this amount is to fill a one cup measuring cup to ¾ with water and put the butter in until the water comes up to one cup. Voila!)

1 cup dry white wine or chicken broth

½ tsp. salt

¼ tsp fresh ground pepper

1 lb. catfish fillets, cut into bite-size pieces, about 1" square

4 sundried tomatoes in olive oil, drained and chopped

2/3 cup grated Parmesan cheese (Food divas all say to use freshly grated. I fudge here and often use cheese I've bought that's already grated.)

¼ cup chopped fresh dill

Grated Parmesan cheese to put on the table and let people help themselves.

Freshly ground pepper after plating

Directions

Microwave the peppers about 3 minutes on medium. Cook the fettuccine according to the package direction in a large pot of boiling water. I like to put enough salt in it that it tastes like the ocean. After you put the pasta in the boiling water, cook the peppers, pea pods, onions, and shallots in butter in a large skillet until the peppers are tender. Remove the vegetables from the skillet.

Add the wine or chicken stock, salt, and pepper to the skillet and bring the mixture to a boil. Add the catfish. Return the mixture to a boil and reduce the heat to a simmer. Cook uncovered for about 3 minutes. Stir the mixture occasionally. Add the tomatoes and return the vegetables to the skillet, tossing to coat.

Place the cooked fettuccine in a large serving bowl. Add the catfish mixture and toss to coat. Sprinkle with Parmesan cheese and dill. Stir to mix. Serve with Parmesan cheese and pepper. Enjoy!

CHOCOLATE FILLING OR FROSTING

(Had to put this in, because it brings back wonderful memories of making it with my grandmother when I was a child)

Ingredients

8 oz. semi-sweet chocolate morsels (Might want to get two bags if you're like me and find that you eat as many as you put in the recipe!)

3 tbsp. hot water

4 eggs, separate yolks and whites (Some people are brilliant at

---

breaking an egg in half and going back and forth between the two halves until only the yolk is left. I'm not. I use a plastic egg separator I've had forever.)

½ pint of heavy cream, whipped (Before you whip the cream, put the bowl and the beaters in the freezer. Takes a lot less time when you do this.)

Directions

Melt the chocolate morsels in the hot water over a very low heat. Remove the pan from the stove and beat the chocolate mixture for 1 minute. Let it cool. Beat the egg whites until they get to a stiff peak stage. (What I do is put another pan and the clean beaters in the freezer while the chocolate mixture is cooling.) Add the egg yolks to the chocolate mixture, 1 at a time, beating after each addition. Slowly add the beaten egg whites and then lastly add the whipped cream. Refrigerate until chilled. Enjoy!

NOTE: My grandmother split a white or vanilla cake into two layers and used this both as the filling and the frosting. When I'm running short on time, I've also been known to buy a pound cake r angel food cake, split it in half and use the mixture as the filling and frosting. Trust me, this is really good!

ERICK'S SANTA FE BONELESS PORK LOIN
(My husband got this recipe from a friend he visited in Santa Fe and I fell in love with it!)

Ingredients

1 lb. boneless pork loin
4 tbsp. cooking oil
½ cup raspberry chipotle sauce (I use the Robert Rothschild brand and get it at Costco. If you don't have a Costco near you, you can buy it online.)
¼ cup barbecue seasoning rub (The one I use is a mixture of salt, sugar, paprika, garlic, & turmeric, and yes, I get it at Costco too,

but others will work equally as well.)

Directions

Using a sharp thin filleting knife, cut and peel off the thin outer membrane of the port loin. (It's called silver skin and is quite tough.) Rub the barbecue seasoning mix into the pork loin on all 4 sides. Heat the oil on medium-high heat until it's very hot. (Rather than burning your finger by testing it, just flick a drop of water into it. If it sizzles, it's hot enough.) Sear the pork on all 4 sides for 1 minute per side. Remove it from pan. (When I'm entertaining, I do this several hours in advance. If you're doing it ahead of time, after it's cooled, cover with plastic wrap and refrigerate. Take it out of the refrigerator 1 hour before placing in oven.)

Preheat oven to 400 degrees. Place the seared pork loin in a glass dish or ovenproof pan. Cook for 23 minutes or until a meat thermometer reaches 125 degrees. The last minute or so heat the chipotle sauce in a small cream pitcher in the microwave. To serve, slice the meat on the diagonal and put it on a plate. Drizzle the warm chipotle sauce over the pork. Place the pitcher on the table for additional sauce. Enjoy!

TWICE BAKED POTATOES
(I've had and made a lot of them over the years, and this is my all-time favorite!)

Ingredients

4 medium size potatoes
8 slices bacon
1 cup sour cream
4 tbsp. butter
½ tsp. salt
½ tsp. pepper
1 cup shredded Cheddar cheese, divided
8 green onions, chopped, green part only, and divided

1 pkg. dry Ranch dressing
¼ cup milk

Directions

Poke holes in the potatoes with a fork and microwave on a high setting for 12 minutes. Turn them every 4 minutes so they cook evenly. (Cooking time depends on the size of the potatoes, so if you're using large ones, cook until they're soft to the touch.) Fry the bacon until it's crisp. Remove from frying pan and set aside. When you can handle the bacon you can either crumble it with your fingers or cut it into small pieces with a pair of scissors. (I'm a crumbler. My husband uses scissors. Both ways work equally well.)

Cool the potatoes for about 10 minutes. (If you go much longer than that, it's hard to scoop out the insides.) Cut in half lengthwise and spoon out the potato flesh, leaving the skin intact. Place the potato flesh in a large bowl and add the sour cream, butter, salt, pepper, ½ cup cheese, ½ of the chopped green onions, the package of Ranch dressing, ½ of the crumbled bacon, and then slowly add the milk at the end. You may not need to use all of the milk. It depends on the texture of the mixture. You don't want the mixture to be soupy.

Mash the mixture with a potato masher by hand until creamy and well-blended. (Don't use an electric mixer, they'll get mushy.) Scoop the mixture back into the potato skins. Top each one with the remaining bacon, cheese, and green onions. Press the topping down gently with fingers. Line a cookie sheet with aluminum foil. Heat the oven to 350 degrees and bake for 25 minutes. (If the potato skins have separated, you can always fasten them back together with toothpicks. Just be sure and tell people about the toothpicks so no one gets hurt!) Enjoy!

NEOPOLITAN ICE CREAM WITH STRAWBERRY BALSAMIC SAUCE

Ingredients

1 pint strawberry ice cream
1 pint green tea ice cream (if you can't find it, substitute pistachio)
1 pint vanilla ice cream
2 cups strawberries (Remove the stems with a paring knife and quarter them.)
¼ cup balsamic vinegar
¼ cup sugar

Directions

Remove the ice cream from the freezer for about 15 minutes to soften it up. Line a 4" x 8" loaf pan with 2 pieces of plastic wrap, 1 going lengthwise, the other crosswise. Put it into the freezer while the ice cream softens.

Spoon out the green tea ice cream into the bottom of the loaf pan and spread it evenly with the back of the spoon. Make another layer with the strawberry ice cream and do the same with the vanilla. Close the plastic over the mixture in both direction and put the pan into the freezer for at least 3 hours before serving. Put serving plates in freezer.

Strawberry Balsamic Sauce Directions:

Put the strawberries in a bowl and sprinkle the balsamic vinegar and sugar over them. Toss gently and marinate for 2-3 minutes.

When you're ready to serve the dessert, remove the plates and the ice cream from the freezer. Unwrap it and put the ice cream on a cutting board. Run a knife under hot water for a moment and slice the ice cream into ¾" slices. Place a slice on a chilled plate and top with ¼ cup strawberry balsamic sauce. (This is really pretty when it's served.) Enjoy!

Amazing Ebooks & Paperbacks for FREE

Go to www.dianneharman.com/freepaperback.html and get your FREE copies of Dianne's books and Dianne's favorite recipes immediately by signing up for her newsletter.

Once you've signed up for her newsletter you're eligible to win autographed paperbacks. One lucky winner is picked every week. Hurry before the offer ends.

ABOUT THE AUTHOR

Dianne lives in Huntington Beach, California, with her husband, Tom, a former California State Senator, ad her boxer dog, Kelly. Her passions are cooking, reading, and dogs, so whenever she a little free time, you can find her in the kitchen, playing with her dog in the back yard, or curled up with the latest book she's reading.

Her award winning books include:

Cedar Bay Cozy Mystery Series
Kelly's Koffee Shop, Murder at Jade Cove, White Cloud Retreat, Marriage and Murder, Murder in the Pearl District, Murder in Calico Gold, Murder at the Cooking School, Murder in Cuba

Liz Lucas Cozy Mystery Series
Murder in Cottage #6, Murder & Brandy Boy, The Death Card, Murder at The Bed & Breakfast, The Blue Butterfly

High Desert Cozy Mystery Series
Murder & The Monkey Band, Murder & The Secret Cave

Coyote Series
Blue Coyote Motel, Coyote in Provence, Cornered Coyote

Website: www.dianneharman.com
Blog: www.dianneharman.com/blog
Email: dianne@dianneharman.com

Newsletter
If you would like to be notified of her latest releases please go to www.dianneharman.com and sign up for her newsletter.

Made in the USA
Middletown, DE
14 April 2020